Whispers

of a

Small Town

MARY HOUGH

WRITERS REPUBLIC L.L.C.
515 Summit Ave. Unit R1
Union City, NJ 07087, USA

Website: *www.writersrepublic.com*
Hotline: *1-877-656-6838*
Email: *info@writersrepublic.com*

Ordering Information:
Quantity sales. Special discounts are available on quantity purchases by corporations, associations, and others. For details, contact the publisher at the address above.

Library of Congress Control Number: 2021944803
ISBN-13:   978-1-63728-804-7   [Paperback Edition]
                  978-1-63728-805-4   [Digital Edition]

Rev. date: 08/03/2021

For my family. I love you all.

Table of Contents

"Whatever walked there, walked alone"
-Shirley Jackson's *The Haunting of Hill House*

A Long Night

A lilac and orange sky met the tree line and the bank of the shore. No waves, no movement of wildlife disrupted the calmness of the lake. Instead, a reflection of a singular yellow light danced across the water. My neighbors across Claire Lake could see the porch light. Twilight crept up to the swing and left inky shadows around the barrier of trees.

I was innocent before I touched the lake, brought that water to my lips. Never could I return. The taste of the Earth from this town tainted my lips. The opportunity was there, and I could have left when Magnus refused to stay. What I didn't anticipate was that I would grow roots here. I didn't expect to survive. I tasted the fruit, and I was stuck.

The cool glass of BlackBerry Merlot chilled my palms. Fingerprints left my identity across the stained glass. My identity lingered on the surface of an object containing the solution to temporary amnesia. Unfortunately, I never drank enough to wipe away the flash of memories completely.

I took the last sip and eased myself into the porch swing. It was time. Within reach sat a book wrapped in ribbon cord to bind a leather journal. I rubbed the frayed end of the ribbon between my fingers. A long night lay ahead. A million thoughts to be sorted. *Why do people stay in Claire Lake? Why should I remain in such a place?* Only time can tell.

In purple pen, I scribbled, "Local historians recall a woman who drowned in the lake. She fell in love with a man she couldn't live without. The town's people blame her for the curse on Claire Lake. Once here, one can never leave."

"Is it possible to love one man and not live without? Unrevivable, she was found much later. Her body chewed by wildlife, and her hair matted with seaweed and sticks. Without ceremony, the town's people buried her in a shallow grave, her name etched into a rock nearby— Kathleen O'Leary."

"Locals reportedly saw her walk along the docks near Hotel Claire. Others claim Kathleen uttered curses on those who leave. Some professed she offered guidance." I paused and held the pen to my bottom lip. *I don't buy the ghost stories.*

I questioned aloud, "Why do I stay here?"

None responded.

"I may end things," I wrote.

This Can't Be Fixed

Frank pulled up beside the unknown car parked in his spot.

Moaning and heavy breath escaped through an open window. Frank unlocked the front door and promptly opened it. Moans from outside grew louder and articulated words drew Frank to the living room. *Yes. Yes. Yes!*

Miriam's legs held captive a set of hairy thighs between hers. Springs in the couch creaked with each rocking motion. The man had a fist full of her hair as he lay atop, grinding away. He motioned his groin back and forth. Neither noticed the third person in the room.

Frank dropped his ring of keys to the beat-up wooden floor. *They didn't have the decency to go to the bedroom.* Frank knew his wife's pregnancy did not spout from his seed. It was only a matter of time before the truth unfolded. He hoped that by some miracle, his vasectomy had not worked. Frank never told his wife about the procedure after graduation; his desire to be the last O'Hara to carry the family name. Miriam wanted to pick up after tiny humans, clean soiled butts, and soothe a baby with her lullabies.

The man rushed to cover the bulge that moments ago had been in Frank's wife. Frank stayed in place watching the two. Shook robbed every word—there was so much to say, but he feared only screams would release. Miriam still lay in disbelief on the couch; a clear sheen of moisture lay over her heaving chest as her breast separated slightly to the sides of her body. Finally, she closed her legs and brought herself upright; Miriam refused to look at her husband.

"Hey, man! Have you ever heard of knocking?!" the man yelled, then he continued, "You killed my boner!"

"How strange for a man to come home to his wife after work," Frank said; he cleared his throat and spoke again, "Who the Hell are you?"

"Luke," the man lowered his voice.

"Great, I'll call you limp dick," Frank said and dropped his lunchbox to the carpet.

The insult never fazed him. "Miriam never said anything about a husband," Luke said. The man with a toned body and no signs of hair loss tripped over visibly shaking legs.

The man spoke once more, "I'm sorry, sir! I'm leaving!" He fumbled with the button on his pants as Miriam pulled her crumpled jeans over her thighs.

Frank wanted to break his face with the glass coffee table. But, instead, he jabbed his fingers into the cowering man's wrinkled shirt. "No. Stay. Fuck my wife! I'm the one intruding in this house!" he shouted.

Frank turned away and bounded up the steps two at a time. He nearly tripped over the tear in the carpet. *God Damn it!* Static and the pounding of his blood circulated Frank's deafened ears. He almost missed the unarticulated cries from his wife downstairs. Instead, Miriam's voice broke through his thoughts—through his eardrums.

Frank slammed the door to the bedroom, leaving an indent in the wall from the knob. In the back of Frank's mind, he thought, *I'll fix that later.* Then, in anger, Frank bounced the door off the wall twice more and yelled, "Hey honey, your new man can fix this now!"

—◆—

The suitcase used during their honeymoon to Disney filled, when she finally ran upstairs. Miriam tore through the door. Snot and tears covered her lips.

"Frank! Frank, love! Stop!" she yelled. The slight wrinkles around her eyes and her forehead scrunched as tears flooded her blubbering words. She pulled Frank's packed flannels and jeans out of the suitcase. She balled them up and threw them to the back of the closet.

"Frank, stop packing! You can't leave! Please" she pleaded.

Frank avoided his wife and walked to the balled-up clothes. Then, without folding, he packed them back into the suitcase.

"I don't want to be here with you," Frank uttered. His eyes cast to the worn carpet around the bed. Then, his voice close to a whisper, "I don't want to look at you." Finally, he managed to only look at her tight fists holding their comforter.

"Will you let me talk?" Miriam bellowed.

Frank released the garments held in his tight grip. He closed his eyes and spoke, "Talk!"

"I just wanted a baby! I wanted a baby for us. Never would I have had sex with another man to cheat on you," she said and massaged her fingers over her forearms. White streaks left marks over pale skin.

Frank stopped. "Bullshit."

Miriam paused and eased herself on the bed. "Fine. You're right. You're always right." She threw her hands in the air as if praising God. "Negative test after negative test," Miriam turned to the nightside table, pulled the draw out, and threw it to the floor. Pregnancy tests dumped from the discarded drawer. "Pretty soon, we'll be too old for a baby." Miriam took a deep breath and Frank continued to stare past her. "None of that matters to you. You've barely touched."

His eyes strayed to the ground when he said, "The other day…you came to me with a pregnancy test. A positive one. I knew it wasn't mine." Frank grabbed his deodorant from the dresser and threw it into his bag. Frank stopped and asked, "Where did you find him anyway?"

"Vera found my donor," Miriam murmured.

"Your donor?" a laugh escaped his words. "Leave it to your sister to find a good fuck."

Miriam yelled, "It's not like that!" She paused and lowered her voice, "She just wanted to help us. Vera knew we couldn't afford artificial insemination."

"Miriam! I never wanted kids! I made…" Frank yelled, then composed himself, "I made sure of that a long time ago." He looked down to her belly. "Congratulations."

Miriam wailed, "No! Please, I need your help. I need you!"

"Trust me. It's not me you need," Frank said.

"Don't leave Franky!" she begged. That nickname she used anytime they were intimate; he shuddered.

Again, Miriam balled up Frank's clothes and threw them to the corner of the closet. She screamed as the fist full of clothes landed on the ground.

"Fucking stop, Miriam!" he yelled. Miriam's fingers wrapped around his wrist as he tried to reach his belongings. Frank tugged her feverish hands away. Then, without thought, he shoved her to the bed. In that instant, he looked at his wife. Frank saw the shock that laced her features. Miriam's blond hair stuck to her face in wet strands; the pieces almost covered her wide eyes and raised eyebrows. Her breathing came in ragged exhales as she lay on the bed and rubbed her hand over her still flat belly.

"I'm so sorry," Frank pleaded to her. He jammed his wrinkled belongings into the bag and patted Miriam's leg before she flinched away and pulled her knees to her mid-section. He had never touched his wife in anger before. He had never touched another woman at all before Miriam. Frank swore he could still see his wife's eyes as he darted out of the house and drove away to a secluded campsite by the lake.

Neighbors

We sat in the driveway of our neighbors. I glanced around, not looking at one thing in particular. Gale and Dewey talked; Magnus engaged in conversation as he sipped from an amber bottle. My thoughts scattered.

We lived in a neighborhood between lower-class and middle-class. Claire Lake is the town between manicured inground pools and the blue blow-up-kiddie pool submerged in braided grass and Dandelions. We lived in proximity to people who worked all their lives and received a pension. The residents could comfortably speak on their dislikes of homophobia, race, and welfare in this place. Words flowed and circled our heads like the smoke flicked from cigarettes. *Do I belong here?*

My daughter ran with the kids in the neighborhood. They resembled bunnies as they bounced from lawn to lawn. She blended, Nev spoke their language and grew to understand Claire Lake. Unlike me, she grew up in a place where everyone in town knew her, and she knew them.

I should take Nev to the movies. It's been ages. Maybe after my last hair appointment? That's a long drive for a movie—at least an hour, I think.

Name-brand groceries are a twenty-minute drive away; Sparkle Groceries provided milk, meat, vegetables of the season, and fruit in a Sparkle brand can. The girl at the Kady's Ice Cream talked about a drive-in being built next Summer. Jim O'Hern sold one of his cornfields, but we weren't sure to who. We prayed he sold the property to build a drive-in, but we also knew he sold the property to buy a smaller house.

Magnus bumped my wrist. "Wonder what's going on?"

I pulled myself from thought. I tilted my head. "What do you mean?"

"A guy just stormed out of Frank and Miriam's," Gale said.

"Have you seen him before?" Dewey asked.

"No. Never," Magnus replied.

"They're allowed to have friends over," I said without thought. All looked at me. "What? There's more than just Claire Lake."

"Well, excuse the Hell out of me." Gale shook her head.

"I'm sorry, it's just...there's more..." I couldn't finish before being interrupted.

Dewey spoke above us, "Frank just stormed out. What the Hell?"

"Maybe that guy was more than a friend," Magnus said.

"We don't know that for sure," I said. "They're always fighting."

"Not as much as them." Gale pointed down the street. "I think I can hear Jack and Wendy from here."

We turned towards their house. Sure enough, the couple yelled across the lawn to one another.

"What do you think it's about this time?" Dewy asked.

"I'm sure it's nothing too important. It's not money—that's for sure." Gale turned back to us and lowered her voice. "Have you seen the new addition on the house? It's gotta be worth a fortune." Her voice almost a whisper, "You know he's not raking in that kind of money teaching. So, what does Wendy do?"

Uninterested, I turned back to Jack and Wendy. *Sometimes I wish Magnus and I could yell like that—it beats being passive-aggressive.*

"Look, look, look! Frank's coming back!" Gale reported.

Frank pulled in. He left his car door open, and he ran into the house. We sat there in anticipation. I couldn't help myself; I wondered what was happening. Frank ran back out, this time carrying his lunch box. The car door slammed, and he peeled out of the driveway.

"Now that looked serious," I said, then pulled a cigarette from the box. I inhaled menthol.

They continued to gossip about other neighbors; at the time, I had no interest. Drag after drag, I held the cigarette between my lips. Finally, my eyes wandered to Jack and Wendy's daughter, Hazel. She threw the ball the size of her head in the air. Her arms were wide as she tried to catch. Hazel ignored her parents and focused on the red ball in the air. She giggled until the toy bounced off her head knocked her down. I watched the ball roll into the road. She cried and ran after it.

"Oh my God!" I bolted from my chair, ready to run after Hazel.

I yelled for Jack and Wendy, but they were too invested in their feud. I waved my arms, and then they saw me, but not before they saw Miriam running to the child as well. I stopped near Jack and Wendy's driveway.

"Hazel, get over here. Let's go inside!" Wendy yelled to her daughter.

"Mommy, why doesn't that lady have a shirt on?" Hazel asked.

When the little girl didn't move, Wendy scooped up her daughter. Hazel wailed and kicked the entire way to the door. Then, all attention turned to Miriam. She took a deep breath, covered her breasts with her arm, and walked back to her house. *Now that's strength. I would have run, but she walked. Something serious definitely happened.*

Give Thanks

Frank lay in the middle of the street waiting for Corrine to get off work. He checked his watch. *Jacobs closed forty minutes ago.* He propped an arm under his head and watched the traffic light fade from green to yellow and red. Cold days were soon to follow, but Frank enjoyed the last of the warm nights. *Fall leads to winter, and winter leads to the death of Claire lake.* Most of the tourists fled the area hundreds of miles away after Pumpkin fest. Frank basked in the quiet blanketing the town. *Finally, some peace to be found,* Frank thought.

His fingers ran along with the uneven texture of the road—the scent of tar loitered under his nose. He missed a long day's work and the loud vibrations behind heavy machinery beneath him. Miriam hated the hours he spent away and the dirt buried under his nails. To appease her, he quit his job; he did a lot to calm her.

Miriam seeped into his thoughts again; *then Frank slammed his hand off of the road. Damn it!* It was a year ago when Frank left Miriam; he camped out in Corrine's front yard. Miriam gave birth to her daughter—the daughter she wanted more than him. Poppy entered the world without a daddy. She was supposed to be his daughter; Miriam was supposed to be his wife.

A shadow replaced the traffic lights. Frank's view suddenly cut off when Corrine stood over him with her boots beside his head.

"You know there is a bar up the road, right? One drunk driver could decide to race up here and there you'd be; splat. You just became a human speed bump," Corrine said.

In a population of two hundred, she was the only person he spent time with willingly. She was the only person who didn't ask too many questions.

He glared up at her. Corrine's black locks glinted with red from the glow above, and soft curls framed her face and the bags under her eyes. She peered down at him and tilted her head to the side.

He said, "That's not any different from the human traffic cone you look like." Frank waved his hand to move her aside. "Woman, you're blocking my view and interrupting my concentration," Frank chuckled to himself as she returned the glare.

She returned his glare. "I don't understand... Tourists leave, and you become a nut job. So why do you insist on laying in the road every other night?" she asked.

"If I could afford a chiropractor, I wouldn't be lying here. The road readjusts my spine." Frank cracked his hips.

"You're an odd duck Frank O'Hara. I've never known a person who needed to lay in the road for a good back cracking," she said. The hand tucked in her jean jacket reached out towards Frank and said, "Come on, I'll escort you home. Let's hope the raccoons didn't dump the trash cans again."

"Do you not see that I am busy? I waited for ya, but you left Jacobs too late," Frank said and tried to look past Corrine's glaring eyes.

"Some of us have to work late, but fine." Corrine flipped her hair and continued, "I'll walk home without you." She stepped away.

Frank grabbed her boot. "You've convinced me!" he said and held his hand up. "Since you offered, help me up. My ass is numb." A shiver went through his body when she grabbed his hands with her cold fingers.

Frank dug his hands into his jean pockets once he stood. "I know it's after midnight, but you want a cup of coffee? A warm mug always brings my cold hands back to life."

With a tilt of her head, Corrine spoke, "I've never seen this shade of kindness from you."

"I just hate having cold hands, and yours are like ice," Frank said.

Corrine smiled. "It's late, but a cup of coffee sounds good right now."

Together they walked to the trailer park nestled along the lake.

—⚘—

Most of the porch lights in the little neighborhood shut off hours ago, but Corrine's remained on. Yellow light framing her front door collected moths and gnats. Mildew covered the grass around the yard, and Frank's tent pitched beside the trailer.

"Come on in," Frank said as he motioned to Corrine. "Mr. Dakota gave me the old coffee maker from the break room today," he said and unzipped the tent.

Corrine stepped inside and glanced around. "I must say, I'm impressed by the renovations you made to this place since the last time I was here. I mean, look at this," she said. Corrine pointed to the lamp sitting on the fold-up table. "You're finally shedding light on your little abode."

Frank shrugged and said, "Yeah, I decided to save money on electricity this month. We need to be eco-friendlier. Save the rainforest!" He pulled two lawn chairs from the corner of the tent and set them up at the table.

"Can you please take your boots off?" he asked. "I don't want mud tracked on my clean floors. The maid won't be here until next week," Frank snickered. He turned the LED lantern on and began making the coffee.

Corrine unlaced her Docs and padded over to the empty chair next to Frank.

"As if you could find someone to clean for you. I'm not sure why I tolerate you," she said. Corrine sank into a metal-framed lawn chair and propped her feet on the blue Igloo cooler.

Coffee percolated in the pot and wafted the heavy aroma through the tarped room. Frank sat in a lawn chair and narrowed his eyes. "You tolerate me because I mow your lawn once a week and fix whatever *you* think broke, and I tip you well whenever I go to Jacobs. Besides, you've cleaned my tent before," he said.

She said, "As I recall, I took pity on your ass because you were living in your car. I thought you might sleep better on a cot than reclined car seats." Corrine stood and walked to the fresh coffee; she poured two mugs. Corrine handed one to Frank, and in the other, she buried her nose in steam.

Corrine glanced up. "You could tip better," she giggled.

Steam continued to roll off the mug as her hands warmed up. Everything grew quiet. Frank yawned as the silence outside became infectious. Miriam started to dance through his thoughts; he tried to silence the memories out with song lyrics.

"Frank, you're doing it again," Corrine said, then shook her hand over Frank's face. "I can always tell when you're thinking of her. You are poisoning yourself with thoughts of Miriam."

"It's one of those nights. I can't help it," Frank said.

Corrine grabbed his hand. "I know you can't," her voice softened.

Frank stared down at his worn socks and pulled his hand away. Corrine broke his line train of thought. "As much as I love listening to the scurrying of wildlife creatures outside, I came here for stimulating conversation."

Frank took a sip of his coffee. "Miriam invited me to Thanksgiving," he said. "She wants me to join them for dinner."

Silence thickened. Corrine scrunched her nose and drew her eyebrows. "Are you serious? You're not going, are you?" she asked.

With narrow eyes, he remained focused on a dark corner of the tent. "I told Miriam I would think about it," he said.

Corrine smacked her hand across the plastic of the armrest. "Why? Why would you even consider going?" she asked but didn't expect an answer. So instead, Corrine continued, "You are more gracious than me. There would be no way I could stand to be around her, let alone civil."

An object in motion will remain in motion. Frank watched as her knee bounced.

"I miss my wife," he said, then clarified, "This is the first time being invited back since leaving."

Air leaked through Corrine's exasperated deep breath. Then she spoke, "My opinion doesn't matter because you will do whatever you want, but I still hate her. She was cheap when you married her, and she's still cheap." Corrine rubbed her hand over her brow. "If this will make you a happier, more likable human being, then I support you." she rolled her eyes and sighed once more.

His voice filled the awkward void, "Would you want to come with me?"

Oh dear God. No! I shouldn't have asked. No! Space between the two grew heavy. *Please say no! Please say no!* He held his composure, but his thoughts screamed, *No!*

She simply answered, "Yes."

—⧟—

Frank stood in front of the mirror in Corrine's bathroom. His cleanest clothes hung loosely over his thinning body. He knew that he'd lost weight over the year, but it wasn't until that moment that he thought of his progressive malnourishment. Frank wanted to look his best when he saw his wife, but the image of the man in the mirror did not represent his best. Instead, he looked as he felt, a man living in a tent for a year who was trying a little too hard to impress his wife.

Frank wanted to go home to the house that he and Miriam planned to renovate. He wanted to go back to the bed they made love on for the first time and the bathroom faux marble tiles where Miriam had her first miscarriage. The thought of the kitchen made Frank miss the times he made Miriam her favorite dish of fried chicken on her birthday. Frank missed the memories spent at his house, but more importantly, Frank missed the memories spent with Miriam.

A knock sounded from the thin plywood door before Corrine pushed her way through the entry. She smiled when she saw him. "You weren't at your tent when I got home, so I figured that you'd be in here pampering," Corrine rolled her eyes and continued, "for dinner."

Frank broke his attention away from his image in the mirror. "Do you not know the meaning of privacy? I could have been naked or taking a shit," he said.

Frank grabbed the black-tie from the sink and positioned it over the burnt orange and yellow flannel shirt. Tie knotting was never his strong suit, but he thought today would be an occasion to wear one. His hands fumbled with the fabric. Corrine pushed his hands aside as she stepped in front of the mirror and sighed as her fingers moved over the silky material. She stood close enough that he could smell rose perfume dabbed on her skin. For the first time, he noticed the slight indentation of crow's feet around her dark eyes. He had never seen her look so content with action so mundane.

Frank broke the silence between them, "How did you learn to do that?"

"I used to help my brothers get ready for church when our grandma would take us," Corrine said, then stared off past Frank. "I haven't touched a tie in a while."

In a moment of seriousness, Frank felt tender towards the woman in front of him. He put aside his anxiety about dinner and asked, "Are you alright?"

A small smile melted away the sadness present in the narrowing of her eyes and the curve of her mouth. "Yeah, I'm happy to be going somewhere for Thanksgiving this year. People don't invite me places unless it's for a hookup," she said and squeezed his shoulders.

"I hope our friendship means more than a hookup," Frank teased as he tweaked her nose.

Scrunching her face, Corrine said, "We'd better be going before Miriam decides to disinvite you to dinner. I'm starving!" She checked her hair then walked out of the bathroom.

Something felt off about Corrine. She never talked about her family.

A chill whooshed through Frank's jacket and fluffed Corrine's dress. They stood at the door to Miriam's house. Everything looked about the same as Frank glanced around. The Subaru sat in the driveway, the screen to the front window was still missing, and the handrail still had a broken plank. Satisfaction curled through his insides like smoke. *I can fix this all.*

Frank knocked on the door. Flashes of Miriam's eyes entered his memory, and the thought burned into a headache. *Not today.* Corrine glanced over at him awkwardly but continued to stand straight and look at the door.

"Is she gonna answer the door?" Corrine asked.

Footsteps echoed from inside. Miriam's face lit up when she saw Frank. In a flash, Miriam's expression changed to disgust when she saw

Corrine. Gaining composure, Miriam cleared her throat, "Come in! It's chilly outside." she stepped aside but kept her eyes on Corrine. Miriam spoke, "That's a lovely dress you have on, Corrine."

Frank turned to his plus one and smiled. He hadn't paid attention to the velvet of Corrine's dress or that the shade of red made her silk hair look darker.

Miriam again cleared her throat, "Frank, if you would like to show your guest to the dining room, dinner will be out shortly."

Miriam disappeared down the hallway. Frank glanced over at Corrine and smiled as he led her down the hallway. On the way, he looked at the new pictures of Poppy scattered amongst the walls. A happy child replaced their wedding pictures. Frank ached a little when he saw the picture of Miriam happy. She held her daughter with soft eyes and a tender smile. It was ridiculous, and Frank felt jealous. He couldn't remember the last time she looked at him with infectious joy. Frank dropped his eyes to the floor to avert his eyes from more photos.

Voices from the dining room made him pause. *I thought Miriam invited me.*

Corrine spoke his thought, "It sounds like there are more people here than you expected."

Frank shrugged, "As long as Miriam made a Turkey, I'm happy." The tension in his gut grew heavier as they maneuvered down the hallway and entered the dining room, Miriam's sister. *Damn it.* At one end, Vera and her daughter sat at the table. Vera shook a rattle in front of the babysitting in a highchair.

Frank cleared his throat, "Hi Vera. I didn't expect to see you here today."

Vera's eyes widened for a second before she replaced them with a smile. She stood and hugged Frank. "We weren't expecting you to bring anyone with you either," she said.

"I'm a Thanksgiving surprise, but not quite the surprise that came in August," Corrine said in nonchalance. She found a chair at the decorated table and sat down.

Frank wanted to crawl under the dining room table and die. Poppy was born in August. He smiled and pretended Corrine hadn't said anything.

"Well, aren't we thankful! It's the Thanksgiving surprise!" Vera said and exited the kitchen.

Under her breath, Corrine mumbled, "Bitch I am a surprise."

Frank's hands grew sweaty; he wiped them down his jeans. "I'm sorry, Corrine. We don't have to stay."

"No. You invited me here. Remember?" Corrine asked. She unraveled the napkin holding silverware. She made a show of fanning out the cloth napkin and placed it on her lap. Corrine leaned in and whispered, "Besides, Vera isn't too fond of me. I called bullshit when her husband died. All that insurance money went to her haunted house. I think she still killed her husband to buy that shack."

Poppy slapped her hands on the highchair tray table. Frank sat next to the little girl, but he didn't want to disrupt her. She became a mythical creature he'd heard of but never saw. The pictures in the hallway were true to her character. Frank pushed the ring around the tray to make the child giggle.

"She already has her father's stupid grin," Corrine pointed out. Instinctually, Frank took offense of the daughter that should've been his. For a moment, he believed himself to be the father of Poppy in his house with his wife, and guests for dinner. Frank was the guest, Poppy belonged to another man, but Miriam was still his wife.

His attention pulled back to Corrine across from him. He needed to change subjects. "I like your dress too. I didn't tell you that earlier."

Her face brightened as she looked down at her velvet form. "Thanks! I only wear this dress for special occasions."

The aroma of turkey, potatoes, and yams circulated the room as Miriam and Vera placed the food on the table. Miriam looked between Frank and Corrine as she smiled a little too much. Her face looked tight. "Bon appetite, everyone," Miriam said and passed the potatoes to Frank.

"Should we pray before we eat?" Corrine asked and held her hands out.

"You mean barflies know how to pray?" Vera asked as she scooted further away from Corrine.

With a clatter, Frank dropped his silverware to the ceramic plate. "That's enough! This is Thanksgiving! We're supposed to stuff ourselves until the turkey coma hits!" he shouted.

"Maybe you shouldn't have brought her, dear. I don't remember inviting her," Miriam said. Her smile melted away as she scooped yams on her plate.

"And what is that supposed to mean, honey? As I recall, this is still my house," Frank stated. He piled potatoes on his plate before he grabbed the yams.

"Well, Shnookums, you lost that privilege when you decided to leave." Miriam began to carve the turkey.

"As I recall, I walked into a man cock deep inside of you, babe." Frank gulped down the goblet of Pinot Noir. *This isn't real! I would never talk to my wife like this.* Never in their marriage did he have to raise his voice.

Miriam dropped the carving knife and fork to the table. "I wanted to wait until after dinner, but I want this over," she said and pushed herself away from the table to exit the room. Moments later, Miriam returned with papers and a pen in hand. She said, "I want a divorce." Miriam placed the form in front of Frank.

Divorce, a word to an end. Quiet. The room grew quiet; Frank's thoughts became white noise. The language on the papers looked foreign. His eyes couldn't focus on what they said.

"Eight years of marriage. Eight years, where we built a business together, a home, and a friendship. You killed everything we had," Frank said. He slammed his hand on the table, causing Poppy to cry.

Miriam ran to the child and pulled her out of the highchair. "I loved you so much. I even loved you that night you left. I waited for you to come home, but instead you went to her. I wanted to have this baby with you." She paused. "Frank, I'm doing this for you. It's time for us to move on," she said through tears.

"You're right. It's time for a change," he said. Frank used the pen next to the papers and signed. "This is yours now," Frank said. He took the forms and jammed them in the turkey. Vera's eyes widened as she held the edge of the table. Miriam, too remained quiet.

"Let's go, Corrine. I bet Denny's Thanksgiving is better anyway," Frank said.

Corrine pushed herself away from the table. "Ready when you are," she said.

Frank stopped in the doorway and said, "By the way, I'm taking the Subaru. It's still under my name." Frank linked arms with Corrine as they walked out the door. He held the car door open for Corrine and grabbed the spare key hidden in the driveway.

—⟋⟍—

The food swelled in their bellies. One more bite would have caused chunks to fly. They left Denny's filled to the brim. They drove back to Claire Lake.

Frank glanced over to Corrine. She smiled and said, "You seem more relaxed since dinner. I figured you'd be a lot more upset."

"I feel," Frank thought, *satisfied. I think.* He wasn't sure.

Trees with sparse leaves passed as they drove down the main road in town. Finally, they reached the stoplight at the small intersection. Frank put the car in park and held Corrine's hand.

"Get out of the car for a moment," he said and opened the door. Frank stepped out into the chilly wind. The door remained open as he peaked back into the car and motioned for Corrine to step out.

Like the other hundred times before, Frank lay in the middle of the road. Corrine followed but stood over him. His hand patted the spot next to him. Corrine continued to stand and stare down.

"I'm not getting down there with you. I will ruin my party dress," she said. Corrine swayed her hips to make the ends of the dress flare out.

"Why do you have to be so difficult?" Frank asked. He crossed his arms over his chest as he watched the lights.

"Fine. Pouting Isn't a good look on you. It makes you man child." She lay in the street next to him. The warmth from her body radiated to Franks. His face grew warm as she snuggled in close.

A smirk lingered across his lips. "Was that so hard?"

"I guess I'm becoming a soft touch. I won't say yes to everything," she said.

Frank watched as she stared at the lights. "I would never expect anything less from you."

"I still can't believe that bitch only invited you to dinner to divorce you." Corrine thrummed her fingers onto the road. "If I see her again,

I'm telling her exactly how I feel about her cooking." She paused, "I thought you only came out here to get Miriam out of your head?"

Warmth spread up Frank's arms as he grabbed her hand. When Corrine didn't pull away, he ran his thumb over her knuckles.

Soft hands. Frank never thought of Corrine romantically, but he only wanted to be seen by her. They were alone together. Frank gave thanks for her.

"Let's stop talking about Miriam. She moved on. Now it's my turn." Frank watched Corrine, but she stayed fixated on the lights. She didn't say a word as she nestled closer under the streetlights. They watch the lights fade from green to yellow and red.

White Deer

"Ours was a place of surrender. We'd come home after a long day. Our hands reached above our heads to stretch out the muscles and tension built while away—my legs in "criss-cross-applesauce" as we listened to the stories of each other's day. I sprawled amongst the shaggy red carpet with crayons and books. They were all at my disposal.

"Mom's goulash simmered on the stove. Her intertwining flavors the browned beef seasoned with pepper and salt. Petite diced tomatoes and tomato sauce all did the Nutcracker Ballet over each tastebud. The taste was like nothing else. If a home was food, that was it.

"The crunching of leaves up the sidewalk and Dad's jangling keys alerted the household he was home. With enough love to spread for miles, I met him at the door as he kissed my forehead and handed me his Thermus. Daddy was home. His hairy knuckled fingers curled over my outstretched hands. Mom ushered out of the kitchen and playfully batted at him with a towel to take off his work boots before trudging through the living room. She walked away, but not before he grabbed her butt pocket and pulled her into a kiss. Mom laughed and melted into his flannel arms."

Corrine caught her breath and set her warm beer down onto the varnished bar.

"I thought you said you came from a broken home?" Frank cleared his throat and took another gulp.

"We weren't always that way," she said and flicked her beer cap and gave it a spin. "We had serenity until dad sought out the white deer."

"The Hell is that supposed to mean?" Frank asked.

"My tribe used to tell stories about the white deer." Corrine paused. She cleared her throat and continued, "The elders told stories of the white deer. A symbol for change."

"You can't make me believe one god-damned deer changed your life," Frank said.

"My dad described not a deer, but a woman. He told me that she was the most beautiful creature he'd ever seen." She nestled into her stool.

"It was hunting season. He went out earlier than usual. Dad didn't want to miss the 'good deer.' As he walked the woods, avoided the crunch of sticks and the smell of piss lingering on his camo attire, dad followed a deer all morning. The snow-white coat shimmered in the sun. He lost sight for a moment and then saw her. Dad said she dressed in the traditional regalia of our tribe, glossy black hair, beadwork emulating turquoise strung around her braids, and the purest and whitest buckskin dress he'd ever seen. He was cold, and she saw his shiver. She welcomed him into her wigwam. A fire, warm drink, and blanket were placed for his use. What he didn't expect was to lie with her. I remember him telling me that he'd never loved another woman before my mother, but this enchantress stole his breath," Corrine said. She took another drink and continued, "He fell asleep beside this woman. When he awoke, dad found himself naked and surrounded by nothing but trees. She was gone."

"You're making this up." Frank stood from his seat.

"Believe what you want. The elders also warned us to never search for the deer unless we were ready for a life of unsatisfaction. My dad could have made this up, but he left us in search of that woman," Corrine said.

"Maybe your dad just left," Frank said as he motioned the bartender for a refill.

"He could have. In any case, we lost everything," she said, then finished her beer. "Sugar, do you have a pen?"

The bartender slid her one. Corinne grabbed an extra napkin. She slid the note to Frank.

I can forgive; you should forgive too.

—ᨑ—

She left the bar for the home she dreaded returning to alone. Her car keys felt heavy in her pocket. Like wax, Corrine's winter coat, her snagged beanie, and boots melted away from her body. She stood in the gravel parking lot. Tonight was one of those nights she wanted to feel something, anything—the cold. Rocks and sharp stones dug into the softness of her arch as she walked away down the street. Down a path walked every day years ago.

All remained quiet on the road leading deeper in the path of trees and discarded houses. Her teeth chattered enough to make Corrine wonder if it was possible to break her jaw through shivering. Icy wind and frosted grounds only made the hollowness inside Corrine deepen. She was numb. Pins, needles, and the biting sting of winter's electric shock disappeared. Amputation, the only word she could describe the lack of feeling in her body as she took the country walk. She walked to the place left buried in her memory. As her eyes scanned the dark, her thoughts panned over a collection of memories—the beginning of her pain.

Alone again.

Countryside Walk

Shackled memory of potholed roads and dead trees
Roads wound in a spool of dirt and cow piss.
Dirt embroidered trailer-homes, pass car-washed

Windows

Glance ahead to find the bare fields, frostbitten windows, navy shutters, a house shielded by a tree

Climbed daily

Clawed and climbed desperation surge through
insecure hands,
feeble fingers,

throbbing nerves

This place of pain

Or rather the beginning of true ache

Moment of isolation

THE beginning of adulthood

Permission given to walk past this house meant to be home, the first time in twelve years.

Age does not grace all

Smaller than remembered, garage door dented, splintered banister, dipped roof

Memory ingrained

The night he left, deep ruts in gravel from burnt-out tires, broken nose, discarded child

Tonight is different

When I leave the imprinted images of dad behind with the rest of the ghosts

It still stood. After all, these years of thinking and dreaming of that house, Corrine knew she hadn't made it up. She knew her brain wouldn't shield itself from those fights with her mother in the kitchen, her brothers growing up with sparse food or toys, and the night her dad left.

Corrine stood in the cracked driveway. Discarded sticks and rocks covered the yard. She bent down and held a branch in her fist. *Girthy. Heavy.*

Corrine held the branch over her shoulder as she ran towards the house. Her body and tree went through the front window. Shards of glass flew around the gaping hole. A burning and itchiness attacked her nose and cheeks. She reached bloody fingers to the torn skin and glass etched into her face. Ripples of fire ignited every nerve in her body, heat. She was on fire, and she loved it. There was pain, and there was feeling. She laughed as she pulled slivers of glass out of her pores. For a moment, she stopped thinking about this house and her parents. As she crawled through the windowpane, crunch and shattered glass filled the silence as Corrine crawled through the window.

Her fresh, bloodied footprints lined the path she walked through her old house. New paint, new appliances, new family photos scattered the walls. She wanted to see herself so desperately amongst the smiling family masking her family drama. Her reflection bounced off the glass of the picture frame. She imitated the matching grin found in the picture. A growling, vicious animal lurked within her belly. She was hungry.

The cabinets held more food than ever. *They're not letting their child go hungry.* Corrine pulled her mother's ingredients out and placed them on the counter.

- rotini
- petite diced tomatoes,
- crushed tomatoes,
- tomato sauce,
- burger,
- salt and pepper
- minced onion.

—ɷ—

Just as her mother had made the goulash—the perfect recreation of happier times. Corrine left the mess in the kitchen. *I'll clean it up later.* She held the steaming bowl in one hand turned the faucet of the bathtub with the other. Gently, she put the goulash down on the side of the tub and untangled her body from her bloodied clothes: cuts, bruises, and dirt-covered her feet. Claw marks from the shattered window scrapped her arms and face.

Hot water covered her breasts and belly as she lay in the tub. Goulash kissed every tastebud as she spoon-fed the past into her mouth. She hadn't felt so at ease in so long. Her eyes focused on the water and the dripping of the faucet.

—⟋⟋⟍—

"Mom, she's in the bathtub!"

Corrine jerked away. She spilled the remains of her dish into the chilly water. She looked around, not sure where she was. Her memory was a little foggy. She only really remembered leaving Frank at the bar.

Theo stepped through the bathroom. She wasn't angry; she was concerned. "Corrine, are you okay?" Theo asked.

The fog began to clear. "What happened?" Corrine asked.

"I'm not sure. There's a mess out there," Theo said; she then grabbed a towel from the linen closet and sat down on the toilet. "Here. You have to be freezing."

Images, scattered images, shuffled through Corrine's memory. She broke the window, bloody footprints, and goulash. "I'm so sorry, Theo! I don't know why I came here." Corrine pulled herself from the suction of water. Everything in her body stung and ached. "I'm so sorry!" Corrine apologized. She gathered her ruined clothes and started to put them on.

"Let me grab you something clean," Theo said. She sat up from the toilet.

"No! No. I've done enough," Corrine said.

"Really. It's okay. Let's get you warm, and I'll call Frank to pick you up." Theo left the bathroom. Moments later, she returned with a pair of yoga pants and a crewneck. She offered the clothes to Corrine. "I think these will work," Theo said.

"I'm so sorry," Corrine said. She refused to look at Theo.

Theo softened her voice, "Listen. I specialize in people's pain." She draped the towel around Corrine's shoulders.

"You can tell me about it if you want," Theo said.

"I don't think we have that much time," Corrine said and pulled on the crewneck.

"I can figure something out," Theo said.

I can forgive.

The Other Father

Vera's Jeep bounced over the crumbled driveway to the faded pink house embossed with broken shingles, a splintering porch, and cracked windows. She itched to get started on turning the "haunted house" into a home for her daughter. The house was cheap, and she wanted a new project. The real-estate lady took Vera through the dilapidated lake house property. A voice lured her in and whispered to come closer—a new beginning lay inside. A guiding hand pushed her up the broken stairs, through the torn wallpapered walls and shaggy carpeting. Vera saw potential in the decay. The house needed work, but then again, she did too. The foundation was in good condition, the structure solid. All it needed was a face-lift. Hands were shaken, a deal was made, and the house belonged to Vera.

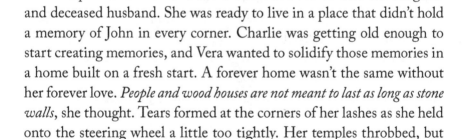

Vera packed the remains of the house she shared with her daughter and deceased husband. She was ready to live in a place that didn't hold a memory of John in every corner. Charlie was getting old enough to start creating memories, and Vera wanted to solidify those memories in a home built on a fresh start. A forever home wasn't the same without her forever love. *People and wood houses are not meant to last as long as stone walls*, she thought. Tears formed at the corners of her lashes as she held onto the steering wheel a little too tightly. Her temples throbbed, but she parked the car, closed her eyes, and inhaled the A/C. She'd decided to move away from the memory of John.

A kick behind the seat reminded Vera, *a fresh start*.

"Momma is this the house?" the little girl asked from behind.

Vera turned to see Charlie stretch her legs and yawn as she arose from her nap. A seat belt mark lay across her pale, freckled face. She yawned; dry drool crusted at the corner of the child's mouth.

Vera soothed, "Hey, baby girl! I was about to wake you."

Charlie wrapped her tiny hand around Vera's extended fingers.

"I'm going to roll down the window, and I want you to close your eyes. Tell me what you hear," Vera said.

The back windows opened as Charlie shut her eyes and scrunched up her nose. Charlie murmured, "I hear," her face relaxed. "I hear water and birds. Are we at the beach?" Eyes wide, Charlie kicked Vera's seat once more.

Vera gushed, "You are correct. Our new house comes with a beach! Momma can teach you to swim, and we can take a dip in the water every day until the weather gets cold." Vera rolled up the windows, turned off the car, and unbuckled herself.

A crappy navy Subaru drove up the tight driveway. Charlie waved when she saw her aunt Miriam step out of the squealing car. The rusted door screeched when Miriam pushed the door open. Curly blond hair blew over Miriam's full tanned face.

"You two made it here in one piece. I was afraid you packed more than what your car could handle," Miriam said as she walked around to Charlie's side. She unstrapped the little girl from the car seat.

Vera stepped into the breeze, moving across the sparse grass and sand. A deep breath overwhelmed her as a homey feeling set in. Vera ushered, "Come on, you two. Help me pack stuff in. There isn't a lot." Vera opened the back hatch.

Charlie strapped a pair of teal goggles over her eyes as she tied her blanket around her neck like a cape. Stray hairs, a pink tutu, and a baby blanket fluttered through the wind as the little girl raced around the driveway in circles.

Heavy tote bags and groceries dropped from Vera's failing grasp when she reached the house. Bags in Charlie's arms released as she ran through the door. "Momma! This is the Pink Palace!" Charlie exclaimed.

Vera started to make a list of the things that needed to be accomplished before nightfall. Her daughter interrupted the thought. "I'm known as the siren of all seven seas. The breaker of hearts by the bay..." Charlie's voice echoed through the living room.

"Okay, my little siren, I need you to dance these groceries into the kitchen," Vera said. She grabbed the bags from the newly cleaned floor. Sweat started to bead around her brow as she swiped her hand across her face.

Charlie ignored her. She turned in circles and said, "We should paint the walls green. Daddy likes that color. I think he likes this house too." Miriam's eyes widened while her hands slid up and down her legs. Vera massaged her temples, *Oh Charlie, not here. Not at the new place.* She closed her eyes and ran clammy fingers through her brunette hair.

"Charlie, stop! You know Daddy is gone...we left him at the old house. We've talked about this," Vera stated impatiently. Puffy pink material on Charlie's sleeves sagged when Vera placed her fingers over her daughter's shoulders. She took a deep breath and redirected her words. "You're right. Daddy would have liked this house. Right now, I need you to go upstairs to scope out your bedroom. Aunt Miriam and I will put stuff away." Miriam remained in the doorway. The temperature in the room surged when Vera pivoted away from her daughter. Charlie continued to sing as she kicked a garbage bag full of swept-up dirt. Particles floated through the rays of light that flooded the living room. The little girl laughed at the falling dust. A speck of light illuminated dirt through the room; it swirled around the floors and into Vera's exposed eyes.

Vera shouted, "Charlie!" Groceries tumbled to the floor once more. "You listen to me, young lady! Get up those stairs right now! I have to clean the floors again!" She yelled. Vera nearly slipped on the loose dirt as she searched for the broom.

Plastic play shoes clicked as Charlie ran in front of her mother with a drooping mouth and scrunched eyebrows. "Momma, I thought you wanted my help?" Charlie asked.

Heat only seemed to rise in the room as Vera fanned herself with her sweaty hands. "I did, but you're distracting me, and I can't focus while you are singing and dancing. Please go upstairs," Vera said.

The child's lips puckered together as she blinked away the beginning of tears. Then, in a tornado of pink tulle, Charlie spun out to the narrow wooden staircase. Vera's heart pounded with the beat of Charlie's plastic shoes slapping across the creaking wooden steps.

Gravity grew heavy on Vera's body as she slid down the wall and looked at the dust piles surrounding her new living room. Her boney knees rested against her chest as she held her face in her hands. Vera wasn't sure how many times she could skirt around the words, "your Dad is dead." Charlie was too young to understand death. Soon, Vera needed to sit down with her daughter and softly tell her, "Honey, Daddy died not long after you were born." Obsession of details started when Charlie found a box of pictures and flannel shirts stored away under Vera's bed.

—ww—

The house almost sparkled when Vera and Miriam got done scrubbing the floors, the walls, and wishes she'd placed in the cabinets days before.

Miriam dropped the broom to the clean floor and slumped to the ground along the wall in the living room. "Is there anything else to do?" Miriam asked. "The house glows."

"No, you can rest for now," Vera said as she crossed her legs in pretzel style and descended to the floor next to Miriam with cold bottles of water.

Crinkling of the plastic bottle crunched under Miriam's hand as she spoke, "So... earlier with Charlie... I think it's time you tell her what happened to John. Moving to a new house isn't going to wash away the memory of him. If she's old enough to wonder where her Daddy is, she's old enough to know why he's not with her."

"Just a little more time. We're in a new house...I'm hoping she lets her compulsion and gravitation towards those stories slow down." Vera sighed. "She knows John almost better than I do. I've told her everything but the drinking problem and the way he died. Charlie is a little girl Miriam. I don't want to stain the image I've created for her."

"Maybe not now, but you will need to tell her. Someday she needs to know John wasn't the protagonist in your love story," Miriam stated. "Maybe she's a little upset that her Momma is going on a date later. What does Charlie think about you going out with her preschool teacher?"

"I haven't sat Charlie down to talk about Jack. Besides, it's not a date, date. We're just having dinner to discuss her transition into kindergarten."

Miriam smirked at Vera. "I'm sure that's all you will be talking about tonight. That is if there is any talking tonight," Miriam laughed.

In return, Vera shoved her sister, forcing the water bottle in her hand to splash to the ground. "Nothing is going to come from tonight. Love is not on the agenda—he's a nice guy who cares about my daughter's future," Vera said.

Her knees cracked as Vera stood. She took to the stairs two steps at a time along the winding path. Charlie's voice echoed from a room down the hall. *Who is she talking to?* Vera slinked around the doorframe to peek in the room. Charlie sat with her dress tucked around her crossed legs in front of the cornered wall.

"I wonder what kind of fish are in the lake?" Charlie giggled and said, "I can't wait to go to the beach." She cleared her throat and shook her head. "Momma said she's going to teach me to swim." Again, Charlie responded and shook her head in agreeance. She spoke again, "The house is nice. I know you like the house too."

Oh God, another imaginary friend. Vera cleared her throat and leaned against the peeling white door frame, "Hey baby girl, who's your new friend?" Vera asked.

The little girl's demeanor changed. She untucked her legs and ran over to her mother and said, "Momma! I'm sorry for messing up the floors." Charlie hugged Vera around the legs.

Through a deep breath, Vera bent at the waist and hugged her daughter back. "It's okay. I'm sorry I got so angry," Vera soothed. "Let's head back to Aunt Miriam's house."

Charlie waltzed out of the room with the clickity-clack of play shoes. An unsettling quiet paired with a chill. *There is no one here—none for Charlie to talk to.* The walls were covered in a tacky seventies green wallpaper with stripes and ovals. Vera couldn't help but laugh and feel disgusted with the people who thought this was a good choice of decoration. The exceptional part of the room was the window seat that looked over the lake. Vera imagined the walls with a fresh shade of purple, the color of Charlie's old room.

Amongst a couple of dolls and a matchbox race car, a picture of John holding newborn Charlie lay on the floor. Vera thought she'd hidden the picture better, but Charlie found it like she always did. She walked downstairs with Charlie's toys while Miriam sang Disney music as Charlie waltzed amongst the clean floors. No dirt to fling.

Vera kissed Charlie's forehead. "Sweetie, you're going to go home with Auntie Miriam tonight. Momma's friend is taking her to dinner, and I need to get ready, but I promise I will pick you up after I finish," Vera said, then turned towards Miriam and whispered, "Keep an eye on Charlie. I think she has a new imaginary friend."

Miriam bit her lip. "Oh no. I'll keep a lookout," she reassured her sister.

Charlie clung to Vera's leg and said, "Momma, I don't want to leave. I want to keep talking to my friend. The one I found when I was upstairs." Charlie grabbed her mother's hand. Vera wondered if the new friend would follow Miriam's. This one felt different from the others the little girl made up. The others were imaginary explorers and princesses animated by her toys. Charlie disregarded all of her toys but instead talked to the corner of the room. Vera feared that this one would end up like the last. Mr. Bunburry was his name; he told Charlie that he had to go away and never returned. Charlie was devastated.

Miriam coaxed, "Come on, kiddo. We're going back to my house for Dino Chicken Nuggets, Scooby-Doo movies, and facial masks." Miriam picked Charlie up started to tickle the child. Charlie squealed and hugged her aunt around the neck.

Vera kissed her daughter's forehead. "I promise I won't be long tonight. Be good!"

—⚭—

The night was chilly as Vera sat on the veranda of the local winery. She wore the new dress she bought and the perfume she wore on occasion. The entire time she got ready, Vera reminded herself that dinner with Jack was not a date. She thought maybe the burgundy dress was too tight. Subconsciously, she pulled it away from her stomach to stretch the material. Occasionally, she would look around at the others who sat with food in huddled conversations. The dark hair falling around her back in curls felt heavy as she maneuvered them from shoulder to shoulder. She rechecked her phone. *Thirty minutes late.* Customers sat at the table diagonal from her conversated ordered appetizers and entrées. All that remained from their date was a lipstick-stained wine glass, and the scattered grape stems from their appetizer. Vera twiddled her thumbs as she looked down at her half drank water glass. She sent a message wondering if Jack was on his way and ordered lemon pepper chicken with a starting glass of Moscato.

An hour later, a message popped up on her phone saying that something came up and Jack would not make it. Mascara coated her lashes and blush on her cheeks. Vera wanted to cry, but that would only give the other patrons something else to look at. *It wasn't a date; It wasn't a date.* She cleared her throat and polished off her entre. Finally, Vera decided, the night wasn't going to be a total waste. At least there was wine and free-thinking Space.

Four glasses of wine later, Vera imagined John sitting across the table from her slurping up forks of pasta. He would have liked this place. She stared down at her plate and thought of how her husband never really cared for garlic bread. He refused to kiss her if she ate it with dinner—Vera took a bite. John was gone, and it was time for her to move on. The picture of baby Charlie and John stuck in her mind. The hazy after-birth memory of John holding her hand and holding their new little girl in his arms filled her tipsy mind. The memories were grand until she remembered the police coming to work. They tell her that her husband had a few too many drinks that afternoon. He drove the car into the lake. Vera took another swig of her glass to banish the thoughts of her dead husband. She remembered holding her one-year-old as they dressed in black and threw dirt on his closed coffin. Maybe it was the wine, but she couldn't suppress the memories. *Please stop. Please, not tonight.*

It was time to go home. Vera texted her sister and asked if she could leave Charlie in her care for the night. *So she didn't have to tell another tall tale of him tonight.* At one point, Vera started to make up stories to hide the fact that her husband died a drunk driver. Finally, Vera paid the check and stumbled to her car.

—◊—

The next day, Vera drove into town. The skies were a shade of grey. Fog hovered like mist over the choppy lake. The car mirror revealed a mess. Vera's mascara coated under her eyes, making her look like the fifth member of the Kiss Band. Makeup from the night before still painted her face. She rummaged through the glove compartment and between the seats, but Vera could find no tissues. Her fingers only made the black smudge further. Vera didn't want to see Miriam looking worse for wear. Finally, an unopened tampon stuck out of her purse; she pushed the soft tissue out of the plastic container and wet the tip between her lips. The makeup disappeared.

Vera could see Miriam sitting behind the counter amongst paint, plaster, and home improvement utensils through the store window. Her plump arms rested next to the vintage cash register as she flipped through a magazine—the bells on the door rung when Vera stepped through the door. Miriam's full lips curved up as she spoke, "Hey Vera! I have the paint and brushes you wanted. I love the mustard yellow color you picked for the living room. The lighting in the living room and the paint color will be very uplifting."

Vera held up the can of paint before placing it back on the counter. "I think it will be too, but I am going to postpone painting downstairs for right now. I want to surprise Charlie and redo the room she picked out last night. Did she seem odd after I left?" she asked.

Miriam pushed her hair out of the way. "Not more than usual," Miriam said, then interjected, "That kid insisted on smudging lipstick all over my face. Why? I don't know." Miriam laughed and continued,

"We played princess and pirates after we did facial masks, and then played a round of Uno. I'm pretty sure she cheated. Nothing seemed to be phasing her."

"No visits from imaginary friends?" Vera asked.

Miriam shook her head. "Not one conversation," she said, then changed the subject. "So…what color are you going to paint her room?" Miriam flipped her blond bob over her shoulder and added, "You know, I have glitter we can add into the paint! We can add the extra sparkle to her surprise."

A smile crept back onto Vera's face. She told Miriam how she had pictured the walls in light and dark shades of purple—a starry night painted on the ceiling.

—⁂—

They loaded the gallons of purple paint, brushes, plastic wrap, and paint stirrers into the back of the Jeep. "So how was last night? Did Jack pay for dinner? Does Jack know that you like to have your back scratched when you've had too much wine?" Miriam asked.

"NO! I drank wine alone after he texted and said that he couldn't make it," the focus remained on the car as Vera spoke.

"What a dick! He invites you to dinner, and then he doesn't show up. Are you going to see him when you start dropping Charlie off at school?" Miriam inquired.

"I will. I intend to be civil with him. We never called it a date, and he's still Charlie's teacher." Vera glanced over at her sister.

"If I were you, I would drop off his end of the school year teacher's present personally. Wear that light blue dress that brings out your eyes and your tits. He needs to see what he missed," Miriam laughed.

"I don't think that is going to happen. But, remember, it wasn't a date," Vera said. Then, she paused and changed subjects, "The reason I'm worried about a new imaginary friend is the fact that I heard her talking to someone yesterday. Charlie is getting attached to the house. I'm glad, but I don't want to go through this again."

Miriam's eyebrows scrunched together. "Did Mr. Whatcha-Call-Him come back?"

Vera shut the trunk. "No. It was someone different. Seeing her talk to the walls in the room made me feel uneasy, but I thought way too much about the new friend last night before bed. It almost sounded like she had an actual conversation. Then, of course, I could only hear her side, but she responded. Before, she only vented to the imaginary friend," Vera's voice wavered. Another imaginary friend made her uneasy.

"Well, you knew that when you moved in, people called it 'haunted house.' So I wouldn't be surprised if there is something there." A guttural laugh bubbled up from Miriam.

"You know that I never believed in that stuff. When I saw this house, I saw something that needed a little TLC. But I'm serious; I'm not too fond of my daughter talking to the walls. This may be a little extreme, but should I take her somewhere and have her checked out?" A deep breath exited Vera's tense body when she spoke. "Should I be worried?" Vera asked.

"You should leave that little girl alone," Miriam said and poked Vera's shoulder. "Those doctors look for something to be wrong, and before we know it, little Charlie will be proscribed a med cocktail." Miriam crossed her arms and spoke again, "I would be worried if she didn't have an imaginary friend. Kids do weird shit all the time. There was this time I freaked a lady out at the grocery store because I told her I couldn't find my brother."

"We don't have a brother," Vera smirked.

"Exactly! I pretended to have a brother when I was little because I wanted another playmate. Charlie has a big imagination. I'm pretty sure she's not going to tell you she sees dead people," Miriam snickered and said, "On the other hand, she could be possessed, and you would finally have an excuse to talk to the new preacher."

"It's the Catholic priests who do exorcisms, not preachers. Besides, I have enough on my plate with this house and figuring out lesson plans for the new school year. So the preacher is going to have to wait," Vera moved alongside the driver's side of the car. She asked, "Why are you so persistent on me enhancing my love life?"

"You've been mourning over John for four years. It's time for you to move on," Miriam said and leaned against the passenger's side of the Jeep. "Well, on that note, you better get a move on, Reverend Yummy

Pants. I hear that he has a baby face and no significant other. You could slip him your number."

"Oh my God. Stop! You can't say that about a preacher! I'm pretty sure we are breaking some law of God just by talking about this," Vera said and put her hand over her eyes to shield her vision of her sister. "Anyway, I'd better go and get started. I'll be back to pick up the rest of the paint stuff later today. I'll pick Charlie up from your house later tonight."

—⚊—

After a week of warding off Charlie, Vera finally decided it was time. The little girl's room was decorated and furnished. She knew Charlie would love the reading nook enhanced with a canopy, string lights, and plush pillows. The starry sky painted above the bed would look after Charlie while she slept. The once ugly green wallpapered walls covered with Charlie's favorite storybooks and purple glitter paint shelves. In the corner sat the rocking chair that looked exactly like the one Vera used to hold her daughter in when she was very small. She couldn't wait to bring her little girl home to her new surprise. Against Vera's better judgment, she hung up the picture Charlie loved so much of her and her father.

—⚊—

The sun fell behind the trees. Lights from distant boat docs sparkled over the lake when the girls arrived at the house. Vera wrapped a scarf around Charlie's eyes as she carried her up the stairs to her new bedroom.

"Momma, what's my surprise. Can I take this off? It's itchy!" Charlie said as she started to pull away from the fabric, but Vera pushed it back over her eyes.

"We're almost there, baby girl," Vera assured. Her daughter walked to the end of the hall and stood in front of the new bedroom. She sat Charlie down and held her hand as she turned the doorknob. "Okay, you can take the blindfold off now."

The smile present on Charlie's face melted away as they stood in silence. Vera pushed her to move forward to look at the room, but Charlie planted herself. "Well, what do you think? Do you love it?" Vera asked.

Charlie ran to the corner and started to knock on the walls. She cried and ran to the walls on the other side of the room. "I can't hear him! I can't hear him!" Charlie screamed. Tears flowed down her face as she looked in her mother's direction. "I can't hear Daddy anymore!" she wailed. Charlie tore the picture off the wall and smashed the glass.

Confusion filled Vera's thoughts. "What do you mean you can't hear Daddy?" Vera asked, confused. "I thought you would like your new room?"

Charlie dropped to the floor and cried, "Daddy talked to me through the green walls. I can't hear him over the purple." She pointed her finger at Vera and accused, "You covered him up. So now he'll never come back! Daddy won't talk to me anymore!"

Vera scooped up her daughter and held her close to her chest. Charlie used little fists to push and punch away from the prison of her mother's arms. Finally, she gave up and relaxed against Vera's chest. Collectively, they both cried as they sat in the rocker. Eventually, Charlie's eyes closed, but her cheeks remained strained from crying. Vera's vision blurred the longer she stared at the soft glow around the room.

She wondered if the hollow feeling would ever go away. The rocking chair slowed the more she thought of her dead husband and her sleeping daughter. Then, under her breath, she called for him; If her daughter could hear him, then she could too.

"John. John, please answer me," Vera called.

She didn't believe he was there, but she called out his name for what seemed like hours. She tucked Charlie into her bed and shut the door as she walked out of the room. For the first time in months, Charlie went to sleep without a story of John.

Hours passed before Vera was able to drift in and out of deep sleep. She felt disappointed in her daughter's reaction. More so, she felt scared that this imaginary friend warped into a fictional dad. Soggy material from the pillowcase stuck to her face as she peeled it away when tossing it under the covers.

In the distance, little feet walked around the creaking of hardwood floors. Vera sat up and rubbed the sleepers from her weary eyes. She was sure that the following day when she brushed her teeth, she would find bags under her eyes. Vera dropped her own bare feet to the floor and immediately regretted it when the cold chill hovering around the house ran up her legs, leaving goosebumps.

The little feet ran past her mother's closed door and down the darkened staircase. Soon the cracking of the flimsy screen door shook the house. Vera threw herself from her bed and slammed her door against the wall as she raced down the stairs, nearly falling on the way out the front door. The sky was clear, with stars shinning in every direction, but it was still too dark to see without a flashlight. Vera didn't have time to go back into her house. She'd heard Charlie race outside, and she needed to find her daughter.

A call from Charlie rang over the sloshing of waves, "DADDY!"

Vera stopped and looked down from the yard and saw the little girl stepping from the wet sand into the lake's water. All air left Vera's body as she flew from the yard to the water. Charlie didn't know how to swim. Charlie's head no longer bobbed over the water's surface when reaching the surface and touching the water. Vera screamed Charlie's name, but she didn't resurface. Vera dove into the ice-cold water. Her body shook violently, but she didn't have time to assimilate to the temp. She held her breath and swam down, down, down. Lack of oxygen burned--her lungs were going to explode. Charlie was still in the water. Before she gave up for more air, a figure bounced off of Vera's. She reached out and felt arms, legs, and fingers; the little girl went limp in her mother's arms as she dragged her to the sand.

Vera gasped for the air she was deprived of seconds before, but Charlie hadn't sucked in the air yet. She lay on the sand, not moving as Vera pushed the water from her daughter's lungs. Water-soaked clothes only tightened the clinging feeling that Charlie may die. Vera pushed and pushed Charlie's chest until a small gasp escaped little lips. Her eyes fluttered open as alarm set in.

"Momma! Put me back! Take me back!" Charlie tried to yell through coughs. Lake water poured around the corners of her mouth.

"What the hell were you thinking?! Charlie, you could have died! Do you know what that means?" Vera asked. She sunk into the sand next to the little girl, staring wide-eyed into the night sky.

"It means that I could see my other Daddy. He said that since you covered him up, I could still find him in the water," Charlie whimpered. She lay in the sand next to her mother.

Vera felt dumbfounded. "What do you mean other Daddy?"

The sand rustled next to her. "I need to go, Momma! The other Daddy from the room is waiting for me in the water," Charlie said frankly. She struggled in her mother's arms. Shivering and wet, but she refused to be held.

"Charlie! There is no other Daddy! There is no Daddy! He died a while ago, and he's not coming back for you or me," Vera cried. Lake water and tears melted together down Charlie's face. "Honey, you have to stop obsessing over this," Vera panted.

"I want to go home, and I want Daddy!" Charlie screamed

"That means you would lose me. Charlie, I would lose you," Vera said, gasping for air. She decided it was time Charlie talked to the new preacher in town or the child therapist. This other father had to go.

Wounded Flower

Miriam lay motionless, curled on the bed. The wet between her legs was still present; she could feel that warmth soaking into her jeans. Frank packed his closet; Luke left when Frank got home—the house was silent, and she didn't like it. All Miriam wanted was a baby. After all of the visits to baby specialists alone, she assumed her husband was the problem. They'd been pregnant before. Still vivid, buried in her memory, is blood pooling down from her wounded flower. The lump of creation, the collected cells that could not sustain breath, remained on the bathroom floor. Oh, how the blood ran through grout between faux marble tiles. All she wanted was to hold that child in her hands as it recognized her voice. *Mommy.*

Miriam sat up enough to see herself reflected in her vanity mirror. What a sight she was; greasy hair from her lovers gripped fingers, and sweat still left a sheen over her exposed breast. When she ran upstairs to her husband, she didn't think of a shirt. In a way, she wanted to be caught by Frank; she wanted her husband to know other options existed. Frank hadn't paid attention to her in two years. Having a baby artificially implanted was out of the question—too expensive. She was trying for a baby with Frank, too painful. After every negative pregnancy test, she could feel her unharvested eggs shrivel like raisins. Those urges that need to be touched at the end of her period, she was done being denied—she missed sex. Miriam longed for the promise of naughty deeds, hands cupped around her breast—hands not her own, and mouths used for anything other than talking.

When Miriam invited Luke to her bed, it was wrong, but she invited him back. She wanted to feel succulent basking in his heat; Miriam wanted to be desired. Her bed was too far away; they made it to the couch. She didn't think about how damn quiet the house would be if Frank found out. As she sat on the bed, all that circulated through static silence was the things she didn't think about. *I didn't know about this; I didn't think about that, I didn't think about him. I didn't think about my child.*

A car door clashed through the loud sound of her breath. Miriam raced downstairs. She gasped uncontrollably; she couldn't get enough air to fill her lungs. When on the ground floor, she used her arm to cover her breasts.

Frank walked through the door. "I forgot my lunch box and keys," he uttered. Frank still refused to look her head-on as he grabbed his belongings and ran out the door.

Miriam stood by the window and watched her husband drive towards the lake. Few neighbors sat in their garages with children and chilled drinks. Instead, her neighbors Jack and Wendy fought while their daughter Hazel neared the busy road with her tricycle.

Miriam ran out her front door to stop the child. She wasn't about to let another little one slip through her fingers.

Anyone outside stopped what they were doing. Wendy and Jack ceased their feud, and the neighbors stepped out of their garages to stare at Miriam.

"Hazel, get over here. Let's go inside!" Wendy yelled to her daughter.

"Mommy, why doesn't that lady have a shirt on?" Hazel asked.

Miriam looked down to see her nipples hardened towards the road. She turned and walked to her front door. She refused to run, and she refused to be ashamed of her actions. Miriam covered her nakedness with her arm and avoided the apparent stares; she was ashamed of her appearance. The cover of a book is everything to these neighbors.

Prudes in public—perverts under the sheets. She thought.

She stepped back into the unbearable stillness of the house. She flipped off the downstairs lights and eased herself onto the couch. That night she'd lost more than she was willing to give.

He's definitely not coming back.

Miriam picked up the phone and dialed Vera's number. On the third ring, Vera answered. Before her sister could say anything, Miriam said, "I'm pregnant, and I regret it."

Past Bedtime

We're curled up on the couch of our new house. Boxes stacked everywhere surrounded my sleeping family. Hours before, we found the DVD player and leather case of movies. Magnus and Nev fell asleep in my lap—I watched the credits roll. Both of my loves breathed deeply. I looked around the room, but nothing held the time. *Definitely past bedtime.*

Crazy how things work out. Nev was four when I almost threw our family into divorce court, and a custody battle. I may have ended things.

—⚬—

One drink lead to laughter. Two drinks lead to flirtation and my hair flipped over my shoulder. Three drinks lead to touching your hand "accidentally;" I want to know if you give the same tingle in my chest— the one Magnus used to give.

You stop my breath.

Four drinks, my thoughts wonder from lips that make me giggle, then down the button up you wear. No lost buttons. Has someone ever taken away those buttons? Have they ever been tore away from your jeans? Five drinks, you say something that makes me question, are you flirting too?

I wonder if you spilled enough courage from your bottle. Do you mean those words? Are you a man of your word, or are you waiting for me to ask? Are you awaiting a nod or a verbal "yes?" You know, I have more to lose than you.

Drink six, you touch my bottom lip. You said I had a drop of drink there. Lucky for you, I can feel every ridge of your print. That thumb of yours remains on the tenderness of my lip. I kiss it. I taste your salt.

Drink seven, you kiss me back.

Drink eight, I like your kiss so much I call a taxi to take me home. You offer to take me home, but I know we'll never make it. I decline your offer—your touch. My husband is waiting; I kiss you one last time before I leave, but I think of you the entire way. I thought of your thumb and those buttons until I see Nev asleep on the carpeted steps inside the house. Her blanket curled under her chin—the front door never wakes her.

I sit on the steps and pull her into my lap. She wakes enough to ask, "Mommy, will you rub my back?"

My hand chilled from outside runs over her Little Mermaid pj's. "It's past bedtime."

She murmurs in my ear, "Will you cuddle with me?"

I kissed her cheek. She curls into my body as I carry her upstairs. I choose her bed instead of his.

—⟞⟝—

Nearly ten years later and Nev still curled close to me. I ran my hand through her mess of brown curls, then rubbed her back.

I whispered to her, "It's past bedtime."

She awoke enough to ask, "Will you rub my back a little more?"

I could have lost her that night; I could have lost Magnus, but I still think of buttons and your thumb.

A Change in the Lake

"The clouds fill; dark and thunderous skies shade the town away from the sun, away from view from above. Heavy droplets of condensation land on the pavement in the street, touching the cheeks of strangers. The water drains into the sewer—spilled into the nearest body of water. As the lake changes, so do the people. We change with Claire Lake, but like the water, we never leave," I noted in the journal.

My glass was nearly empty as I wrote those words. Yesterday feels like ten years ago, but ten years ago feels like yesterday.

Soft Incarceration

Note to self: Write this story in third person; create distance. Tell mom's story; that's what's important.

I readjusted myself on the swing. My body creaked with the chains. *How do I write about Mom?*

—m—

Her fingers froze as she brushed off the car. No use. The powder falling continued to cover frozen sheets of sleet. She only had a few minutes this morning to wake up, shower, and grab a hot drink. Theo could feel the tips of her hair turn to icicles. *Stupid alarm! Why didn't it go off? I knew I shouldn't have washed my hair this morning.*

Theo looked across the street; she could barely see her neighbor's house. The snowplow had not rumbled through the road in hours. An ache echoed through her abdomen. *I'm not going to have time to stop for breakfast.* It was decided, she would have to reschedule her morning appointment. Vibrations announced a call, and Theo dug into her coat for her phone.

Moments passed; a lifetime passed. Then, finally, she dropped her phone back into her pocket and ran to shovel the snow off her car.

—m—

Paralyzed in waiting, we waited for news of progression. Finally, a month passed before Saoirse was released to go home.

Through the kitchen window, Theo watched as squirrels leaped from tree to tree. Another hot day. She gathered up the food tray, a glass of water with a bendy straw, and the morning paper. Saoirse was still resting from her sleepless night of asking, "Where's Dad?" "Where did everybody go?" and her pleas for help.

I need to get melatonin.

Saoirse's blankets left astray around her body. Theo repositioned the blanket over her legs and put the tray down across Saoirse's lap. She pressed the button to raise the head of the bed. "Good morning, mom," Theo whispered. "It's time for breakfast."

Saoirse opened her eyes one at a time. A scowl crossed her face when she looked from Theo to the food on her lap. "I'm not eating this. You eat it," Saoirse groaned.

"Mother, please eat. I need to give you your morning meds," Theo pleaded. She sat in the chair next to the bed and interjected, "It's a good thing we're not going anywhere today. It's so nice out. Maybe later, I can wheel you out to the porch." Theo grabbed the water and bent the straw to fit Saoirse's mouth. As usual, she refused to drink.

"Mother, you need to drink. The nurses probably think I am neglecting you." Theo tried again, but her mother refused. "Your pee is brown," Theo emphasized.

"I will not wet or shit in this bed anymore. Now, take me to the bathroom!" Saoirse hollered.

"Mom, you have two broken ankles. We're not going anywhere. That's why you have pads and a catheter. Just go," Theo said. She peeled a banana and broke a piece of it off. She held it to her mother's mouth. A moment later, the chewed banana was spat in Theo's face.

"I can't do this right now," Theo cried. Banana covered her lashes. She wiped the remaining banana from her eyes and left the room. Her fingers stung, heat rose in her face, and tears dripped from her eyes. Finally, she collapsed on the floor by the coach.

"Help. Oh, God. Help me!" Saoirse screamed from her bedroom.

Magnus ran from the kitchen, holding his travel mug and briefcase. "It's like I walked into a burning barn this morning," Magnus joked. Then, he bent down to Theo's level. "What happened?"

"She refused to eat," Theo sobbed.

"Well, that's normal." Magnus gave a slight smile. "She's always like this at mealtimes."

"I know!" Theo scolded. She glared at him and said, "Sometimes she's a lot to handle. Unfortunately, today is one of those days."

"It wasn't my idea to move her in here with us," he retorted. Magnus readjusted the handle of his mug and added, "There are places that would take care of her."

Theo stood. "Are you being serious right now? Are you suggesting that I would put my mother in a home?" she asked.

Magnus sighed, "You can't do this on your own. She is more than you bargained for."

"As I recall, there are three people who live in this house, but only one takes care of her," Theo argued, then took a moment to collect her thoughts. "I wasn't always what my mother bargained for either, but she always took care of me. That lady is perplexed and in a lot of pain. I will do whatever I can for her."

"Okay," he surrendered and put his mug and briefcase down, and hugged her. "I hate seeing you like this. It's not like you to stretch yourself this thin."

"I don't want to fight with you," she said and hugged him back.

"I don't want to fight with you either, but you haven't been *you* since we moved her in."

"She's my Mom. I'm the only one who can take care of her." Theo picked up his stuff and handed it back to Magnus. "Now, go make us some money. You're the one bringing home the bacon now," Theo laughed and ushered him out the door.

"It's weird being the sole breadwinner. Now I have a stay-at-home wife, dinner on the table when I get home, and fresh-pressed laundry," he yelled from the driveway.

"Just for that comment, I'm scrubbing the toilet with your pillowcase," she called to him and blew a kiss.

—⁂—

Mid-afternoon sun seeped through the blinds of Saoirse's bedroom. "Theodora, please come in here," Saoirse begged. "I had an accident."

Theo figured as much. A plastic basin of hot water sloshed to Theo's arms and chest. "That's ok, Mom. We'll get you cleaned up," Theo soothed. She put the water down and shouted from the door, "Nev, I need your help!"

"Coming!" Heavy footsteps made the ceiling creak. A moment later, Nev came in the door.

"What are we doing, Momma?" Nev asked. She pulled a hair tie from her wrist and bunched her hair into a high ponytail.

Theo grabbed the flushable wipes, a washcloth, and fresh bed pads from the nightside hutch. "Help me roll her on her side so I can clean her butt," Theo instructed. She moved to the backside of the hospital bed and lowered the bed rails.

Nev held Saoirse's hand and ran her thumb of veiny thin skin. Then, Nev spoke quietly, "Look at me, grandma. Roll towards me." She gently pulled Saoirse's hand and placed it on the bed rail. Theo pushed her back and began to roll her.

"No! Don't do that," Saoirse screamed. "You're trying to kill me! I'm going to fall!"

"Grandma, you're ok. I'm not going to let you fall." The teenager soothed the older woman.

"Don't touch me! Don't touch me!" Saoirse yelled and continued to scream, "Dad!"

Nev continued to shush her grandmother, and Theo wiped away excrement. The smell still made Theo squeamish, the scent of fermented Hershey Kisses rolled in maggot-infested meat. She wanted to comfort her mother, but she also wanted to clean the mess as soon as possible.

They placed the clean pad over the lift harness under Saoirse. Theo cleaned the remaining waste from around the catheter and between her mother's legs.

Nev tied up the whole garbage bag. "Momma, what do you need me to do next?" she asked.

"Can you put her blankets and sheet in the washer? Can you also grab me a clean blanket and sheet to put on her when we're done?" Theo requested.

Her daughter nodded and left the room with the soiled bedding. Theo removed her mother's hospital gown and squirted body wash onto a wet washcloth. "As soon as we get you cleaned up, we can go outside," Theo said.

"Huh?" Saoirse asked.

Theo spoke louder and slower, "We can go outside after we get you cleaned up," she exaggerated and cleaned around her mother's breasts and belly.

"There was a time, you know," Saoirse spoke quietly, "I used to have nice breasts." Clarity struck Saoirse.

"I know, Mom. You tell me every time I bath you," Theo said and rung out the soapy washcloth.

"Your Dad wasn't the only one to tell me."

Theo stopped mid-wash of her mother's belly. "I thought Dad was the love of your life?" Theo questioned.

Saoirse's voice grew soft, "He is. When your Dad left for the navy, I wasn't sure if he would come back. You were little."

"Mom, I don't want to hear this," Theo replied and sat back in her chair. She listened anyway.

"A few of my friends took me out for the night. They knew I needed a night away. So, grandma babysat you. Then, we went out to a bar in Pittsburgh," Saoirse said.

"Oh god, mom," Theo interjected. A deep breath held tight in Theo's throat.

"We drank and laughed, then all of a sudden, the bar opened up with people cheering. I turned to see what was going on, but the cheering people came towards me. They weren't looking at me, but they were all looking at the man who sat next to me. He was looking at me."

Theo, still holding the washcloth, dropped it into the plastic basin. "Who was he?" she asked.

"If I told you, you would never believe me," Saoirse smiled.

"You've gotten this far. You have to tell me."

"My friends and I knew that a concert was happening in the city, but we didn't think anything of it," Saoirse paused, then continued, "It was Freddie Mercury."

"No. There is no way!" Theo insisted.

"It was him. He looked as he did in pictures. As soon as the noise began, it stopped; all I heard was his voice. He asked if I minded that he sat there. I, of course, didn't mind. For the rest of the night we talked, he told me how Queen wrote their songs and the electric surge he felt every time they performed in front of a crowd," Saoirse said and leaned back into her propped-up pillows.

"What happened?" Theo asked, then crossed her ankles and arms.

"Well, I said goodnight to my friends, and Freddie escorted me to my car. His security must have kept the crowd at bay because none disturbed us. He got into my car with me, and we kissed. At that moment, I felt so guilty and relieved to be noticed. I let him touch me, but no more than that. In the end, he told me that I had a nice breast, and we parted ways. When I got home, I just held you and cried. What I did was wrong, but it felt good. A couple of months later, I got a letter from your Dad saying he was coming home. I never told him or anyone else." She closed her eyes.

"You never told Daddy?" Theo asked.

"No. No one," Saoirse said.

"Why?" Theo questioned.

Saoirse turned her head. "At the time, I didn't know what I was going to do. I had a screaming daughter who only asked for Daddy. I worked until I was too exhausted to move to cover all of our bills. At the time, I thought of ending things," she paused. "He helped me understand that I had someone to return to. You."

Theo had no words other than, "Momma." Theo dried her mother off and placed a clean hospital gown on her.

"Nev, I need a clean blanket!" she yelled to her daughter.

Another month gone. Another memory lost. Another day asking if the end is near. Theo could feel the grey growing out the pigment of color. She could feel her body's age—the beginning of arthritis, constant nag of joints if she sat the wrong way, and a growing headache from lack of sleep. Theo could only sleep if Saoirse happened to fall asleep. There was not enough Melatonin or Tylenol PM to knock out the older woman. Every day felt like Ground Hog day—never-ending, the same screams for dead relatives and the dark flow of excrement. Every day Theo thought, *home. She needs to go to a home*, and then guilt settled in; *I'm the only one to take care of her.*

I may end things.

—⚍—

The end of summer neared. Saoirse's mind wandered further and further away.

"This house is bigger than your old one," Saoirse said. "No one's broken in?"

Theo set her ice tea down. "Mother, Corrine is a friend. At the time, she needed help," Theo added.

"I heard she's pregnant," Saoirse said.

"Where did you hear that from?" Theo giggled, "You haven't left this house in months."

"My visiting nurse." Saoirse lowered her voice, "Minxy said Corrine was asking about prenatal vitamins the other day."

"Those vitamins are used for more than babies," Theo stopped herself, then asked, "Are we going to gossip or play cards?"

Saoirse pointed to the shuffled deck. "It's your deal," Saoirse said.

"Two-handed Euchre?" Theo asked.

"I'm not playing War," Saoirse joked.

—⚍—

The score was eight to nine. Theo only needed one point to win. Saoirse won enough tricks to win the game, but Theo wasn't about to let her mother win the whole hand. So she put down her last card in defense, Jack of Clubs. A grin on Saoirse's face melted away Theo's victory. On top of the club was a Jack of Spades, a card worth slightly more than Theo's.

"Mother, you have beaten me again," Theo said and gathered up the deck and placed it back into the box.

"You can't beat seventy-two years of practice," Saoirse said as she took a sip of her ice tea.

"I know you learned from Grandma," Theo said.

"Is your Dad coming to pick me up today? I think I'm ready to go home," Saoirse sighed.

Theo held her mother's hand and gently squeezed. Then, she soothed, "Mom, Dad is dead. He died 15 years ago."

The old woman yanked her hand away. "Theodora. Do not lie to me. I talked to him this afternoon," Saoirse hissed.

"No, Mom, you didn't," Theo pleaded.

"Yes. I did. You didn't see him when he dropped me off," Saoirse growled.

"Whatever, Mom. Just relax. Enjoy being outside," Theo said.

"By God, I'm never coming here again." Saoirse mumbled, "Bitch."

"Just relax, Mom," Theo sighed and continued to ignore Saoirse's ranting.

The women continued to stare out at the landscape before them. Birds dipped below the porch's roof, leaves turned towards the sky praying for rain, and gnats swarmed in spots of the yard. The warm air under the shade of the porch roof brought Theo the feeling of nostalgic summers past; orange slushies fresh from the blender, late nights among fireflies, and her mother's yellow dress she wore to the grocery store. Theo's eyes grew heavy as she nestled into the wicker chair; she could feel her thoughts drifting to childhood. A delicate cool fell to Theo's hand. She rubbed the object in her hand, and she could feel a chain between her fingers.

One at a time, Theo opened her eyes. Again, she looked in her left hand to see gold glisten in spots of sun seeping onto the porch. This time, with both hands, she held the necklace. Hung from the chain was the Black Hills Gold rose pendant. Theo remembered sitting on Saoirse's lap as she had the rose between her fingers.

"It's yours," Saoirse offered. She folded her hand around Theo's and said, "I've meant to give this to you for ages."

Theo couldn't help but watch the glisten from the necklace. "Momma, this is the necklace Daddy gave you," Theo said.

"Now it's yours," Saoirse noted. She pulled her hand away and nestled into her wheelchair.

Screams erupted once again. No room could deny Saoirse's cries through less than paper walls. Theo hadn't slept in her bed in months—the couch's leather began to crack and break off; there was an indent for Theo's head. She pulled the blanket from her body and threw it to the floor. Everything hurt as she slowly stood and walked to her mother's room. Sleepers crusted the corners of her eyes and coated her vision. Theo felt like a child going to her mother's room late at night after a bad dream.

The night light illuminated Saoirse's naked body, and the blankets were tossed to the ground. As Theo did every night, she picked up the bed coverings and rearranged them over her mother's exposed legs. She sat in the chair by the hospital bed.

"Momma, settle down," she softened her voice. "Go back to sleep."

Saoirse's eyes remained closed as she howled, "I fell! Get me off the floor!"

"Shhh…Mom, you have a bad dream," Theo soothed. She started to hum a lullaby as she leaned her arms against the bed rails.

Saoirse's eyes opened. "If you get near me, I'm going to hall off and hit ya!" the woman yelled.

"Mom! Stop it!" Theo shouted over Saoirse's screams.

Saoirse turned her head towards her daughter, "You did this! You did this!" she hollered and slapped Theo's arms away. "Get your Dad! I'm going home!"

"Momma, you are home. It's late. We're not going anywhere!" Theo yelled.

"I'm not staying with you! Get me the Hell out of this bed!" Saoirse screamed.

"We're not going anywhere!" Theo yelled.

"Take me outside. If I stay in this room one more second, I will die." Saoirse continued, "I will kill myself!"

"Fine, you want to go outside? We will go outside," Theo stated.

Theo grabbed the lift and hooked the straps on the harness. Saoirse lifted from the bed; excrement oozed from the harness. *I don't care right now. I'll clean her later.* Saoirse continued to scream about pain, her hair being messed up, and the shit exiting her body. Theo would take care of it later. *This is not Mom. This is not Mom. This is not Mom. I may end things.*

Theo wheeled her outside to stare at the lake. She thanked God there were no neighbors close enough to hear her mother's screams. As soon as the piercing pitch to Theo's eardrums started, it ended. Saoirse calmed enough only to mumble. Theo sat on the porch swing and wrapped her nearby blanket around her body to fight off the chill coming from the lake.

—⟋⟍—

Morning sun and heat arose Theo from asleep. She wasn't sure how long she'd conked out. More sleepers coated her eyes; she rubbed them away and pulled herself awake. She looked across the porch. The wheelchair was empty.

Theo immediately stood, her heart pounded in her throat and her breath taken away. Saoirse lay by the lake—her body scrunched as she lay face down in the shore's sand. Theo jumped from the porch and ran to the water. *She must have crawled.*

Water had not yet lapsed over her mother. Theo flipped Saoirse over to find the faint rise and fall of the old woman's chest. This was the calmest her mother had been in what felt like a lifetime.

"This is my fault. I promised to take care of you," Theo whispered. "I fell asleep. I shouldn't have brought you outside." She cradled her mother's head in her lap. They sat there for a long time.

Saoirse finally stirred. She mumbled, "Did I reach the water?"

Theo looked down. She hadn't realized she was crying, but tears fell on her mother's face. "Yes, Momma. You reached the water," she reassured, "but I'm not ready for you to go in yet. Claire Lake doesn't need you yet. I need you." They continued to sit on the sand as the early morning sun sparkled across the waves. Theo hadn't realized how beautiful the lake could be.

Mother Knows

"My name is Wendy, and I'm an alcoholic," Wendy said before her AA group.

—◊—

"I'm sorry, miss, but do you have underwire in your brassiere?" the white-haired CO's said, his tone was stern.

Hazel felt around the bottoms of her breasts. "Yes sir, I do," she said, the heated rose in her cheeks. The other CO behind the desk, fresh with a smooth forehead and welcoming smile, tried to recover a slight chuckle with a half-hearted cough.

Jack impatiently pulled on the loose thread above his jean pocket until a tight noose cut the circulation off the index finger. He let go and folded his arms over his chest. Jack didn't want to visit Wendy today, but Hazel insisted. His daughter remained behind the metal detector.

"You must pass through without setting off the alarm, and I can't grant you access to the visitor's area without a brassiere," he said.

Jack assumed the line was used at least a thousand times a day on visitor weekends—Hazel's mortification did not faze the CO. *Who even says brassiere anymore?* Brassiere- the word felt foreign on his tongue as each syllable bounced through his thoughts. *Bras-siere, brassiere, braaas-siere.*

"Sorry, sir, we'll be right back." Hazel grabbed at her father's arm.

She pulled him from the banquet of thoughts. Outside the prison's public doors lay the black pool of heat-soaked pavement.

"We don't have time to go back home. I have a meeting later with the parents of my students," Jack grumbled, then pressed his remote, and lights from the family Jeep chirped to life. The headlights flashed with the remote to unlock the doors.

Hazel climbed into the front seat. "You just want to see Charlie's Mom. No one should be that excited for a PTA meeting. Besides, I have an idea," she said.

He opened the back hatch to check if his daughter had a discarded wireless bra in the back. Jack rifled through fast-food wrappers, plastic water bottles, and blankets that had not seen a washer in months. "I don't see anything back here for you to use. All I see is garbage," he said.

"Dad, I'm not making a bra out of old cheeseburger wrappers. I told you, I have a plan." She unhooked her bra and pulled the straps one by one from her short sleeves. "Do you have a knife or something?" Hazel asked.

Jack closed the hatch and made his way back to the driver's seat. By then, his daughter found a Philips screwdriver and began to cut the underwire out of her bra. Jack huffed, "Is this necessary? We do not have to see your mother today." He felt defeated by Hazel's insistence. Jack turned on the ignition and fanned the AC into his face—the car felt like a thousand degrees, and he felt a nervous shit-stirring in his abdomen.

Finally, the first wire broke through the nylon material. She spoke through gritted teeth, "I accept every phone call, we write letters to one another, I send pictures, so she doesn't forget our faces. The books stacked up in her cell are what I bought to fight her loneliness."

"Your mother would not have been lonely if she'd kept her promises to you. She wouldn't be sitting in the cell block staring at the cracks in the wall if she'd kept her promise to me," Jack stated.

Hazel paused, cutting into the ruined bra. "What did she promise you?" she asked.

"Nothing. It's not important anymore." He opened the car door and decided he'd rather drown in the heat.

"Terence! Inmate 62389, your family is here to see you. Look alive," the female guard with shoulders built like a line-backer bellowed through the bars. Wendy had just fallen into her usual morning coma.

The dreams floating in her headspace during that fifteen minutes were sweeter than the news of her family's visit. Wendy pushed the recent scattered photographs of Hazel and Jack smiling amongst the others from *father and daughter dates* under the bunk. Without much rush, she threw on the navy-blue jumpsuit designated for visitor weekends. She'd never worn it before—the fabric scraped her skin with *any* sudden movement.

On her way out of the cell, she accidentally knocked over a stack of books recently shipped to her from Hazel. She didn't have the heart to tell her daughter that books weren't going to fight the guilt she carried when Hazel's existence caused the shame. *She needs to save her money.*

Wendy thought back to Wednesday's AA meeting during the long walk across the jail—after 15 years of tight-lipped secrecy, she finally revealed what made her drink. What else was there for her to do? So Wendy told the story not found in books but only through word of mouth...

The visiting room was nothing like the sitting areas pictured in serial killer documentaries; Jack and Hazel sat in the stiff plastic chairs. There were no metal tables with prisoners chained to a bar. Instead, a corner of the room was dedicated to children—building blocks, puzzles, and crayons lay in shambles amongst primary-colored foam play mats. Stretches of plastic orange chairs lined the room in rows. Inmates waiting for loved ones scanned the windows running the length of the wall. They looked like sleep-deprived passengers waiting for their connecting flight to a country on the horizon. Mothers braided the hair of their children while they reminisced about life outside the razor wire. No doubt Hazel recalled the quiet moments of Wendy while she watched children climbing over their mother's laps. Wendy never held their daughter as she could lose her. Jack thought he knew why.

A male guard stood before the woman. "Line up inmates. You know what to do," the correctional officer yelled.

Wendy, among the other ladies, lined the wall before entering the visiting room. The girl next to her, not more than seventeen, spread her hands on the wall and her legs separated. Wendy tried to keep her eyes towards the cement wall; the guard ran his hands over her breast and between her legs. His hands lingered longer than necessary.

"You're filling out that jumpsuit," he said.

Through gritted teeth, she said, "You know why." He flipped her around and held her hands behind her back. The Co motioned for another guard. "Take this one back to her cell. She talked back!" he bellowed.

She thrashed and resisted the grip of the guard. "No! My son is here!" she hollered and continued to scream as they pulled her away, "I need to see my son!"

Behind Wendy, she could feel the co separate her feet farther apart. "Now, you're not going to give me any trouble, are you?" he asked.

Wendy continued to stare straight ahead. "No, sir. No trouble," she insisted.

"Good," he said. He patted her down and sent her in line with visitor's papers.

A guard packing a nightstick opened the door and led in a line of ladies one by one. Each carried papers revealed their last names, inmate numbers, and visitor's list. Some gave a small pep to their step as the guard unlocked their handcuffs—they had families and children waiting. Wendy walked in the rear. Jack didn't see her face right away, but he could see the gloss and unruly red curls bounce at the back of the line. Communication with his wife was cut off altogether six months ago when she officially was sentenced to ten years minimum and twenty years maximum in the state prison for women offenders. It was eight months ago Wendy totaled the Subaru and t-boned another car. He made divots in his jeans with his chewed-off fingernails; the nervous shits returned.

Finally, Wendy gave her papers to a CO and walked over to her family. Wendy's face revealed the same churning feeling Jack felt in his gut. Hazel spoke first, "Hi Momma."

Wendy was slow to the hug, but eventually, her arms wrapped around their daughter. Jack left a peck on his wife's cheek; it felt like kissing a stranger—no feeling. He could see the last fifteen years written all over her face after his kiss, years of disappointment. In the previous five, Jack started a list of why Wendy acted so vanilla towards him and distant from their daughter. He ran through the list again.

1. Wendy not finishing college, but he did.
2. Dropping out junior year to raise a baby.
3. Marring him.
4. Then her poor attempt at being a stay-at-home mom.

Wendy resented her family for the life she never got to have.

"Hi, my name is Wendy, and I'm an alcoholic." None appeared too interested, but the six other ladies sitting in the circle replied, *Hi Wendy*. She continued, "I landed myself in this cement spa by drinking too much. Being sober for the first time in six and a half years, I've sat down to think about why I liked having a drink in my hand. Well, My daughter." She thought this would be a dramatic reveal in movies, shocking, but none seemed aroused by the news—they were busy picking at hangnails and loose cotton threads.

Wendy shrugged and rolled her eyes. The story wasn't for *their* entertainment anyway—the retelling was for herself. "This is one tale my husband has not heard, and he's heard a lot. Jack and I started dating freshman year. He deflowered me, and I thought I was in love, at least until junior year. Then, like many phases, the lust faded away into a sort of chore. Sex became stale. He was content, but I wasn't ready to settle down. Jack talked about kids with my hair and his eyes—he talked about a house in the country. I wanted plane rides and foreign languages. Everything changed when Jack's older brother Max decided to get his master's in a college that was a hop, skip, and a jump from ours. First, there was flirtation over wordplay, and then there was a physical attraction." Wendy wasn't sure if the sun was branding the rouge on her face or if it was still Max.

Inmate Lupin cleared her throat and coughed a few times.

"Do you mind?" Wendy asked.

Lupin scratched dandruff and ate the pieces from her fingernails. "I didn't realize AA was storytime," she expressed.

"Maybe you wouldn't cough if you stopped eating your scalp," Wendy fumed.

Lupin rose from her chair and threw it. A guard was quick to grab her.

"Get her out of here," the councilor said.

"You'll be back in solitary soon, Terence!" Lupin called as they hauled her away.

—⟋⟍—

Seeing Jack made Wendy want to turn around, crawl to the corner of her cell, and drown in the toilet.

—⟋⟍—

Empty conversation filled the space between Jack and Wendy as they talked over their daughter. The most conversation consisted of: Hi, how are you? Good. The weather can't decide to make up its mind. How are your AA meetings? Good. Jack crossed and uncrossed his knees, Wendy pulled at the choking hazard that became her jumpsuit, and Hazel consistently looked between her parents as if to signal new conversation.

Finally fed up, Hazel stood and walked to the nearest guard. "Sir, can I have the key to the bathroom?" she asked.

—⟋⟍—

Wendy's mind drifted back to AA. "Max was twenty-four, and I was just shy of twenty-one. He bought me liquor my roommates were too poor or too young to buy. I handed him my naivety of sex. Jack made love, but Max fucked." The word *fucked* produced attention amongst the others—an understanding passed through the group. One AA member with grease-streaked blonde hair cheered. Wendy continued, "That semester, I learned more than the theorem of Freud and Jung. It was wrong, but I had the best of both worlds—a man who wanted a future and a man who wanted the moment. The affair curled my toes and begged for a scream until I peed on a stick. Two pink vertical lines, pregnant." Unconsciously, she rubbed her flat empty belly.

"Of course, I thought of all of my options—adoption, abortion came to mind, but I didn't want to get rid of my baby. I liked the idea of a child conceived through a tumultuous time—a child with a backstory. The baby was no bigger than a thought, but I envisioned it as a little boy I would name Danny. I thought of all the traits my baby boy would have from Momma and Daddy. Still, I wasn't ready to settle down, but I saw a future with Max."

She paused and bit her lip, "He never found out. A week later, a grad party and alcohol poisoning led to Max's end. He smothered to death in his vomit." She paused for a moment. Years passed since the last time she thought of Max's death. His demise should have been a cue to stop drinking. She narrated, "At the time, Jack was too grieved to understand why I cried in the shower, before bed, and during sex. Everything reminded me of my child's father. In a split second, I decided that Jack could never find out that the baby was not his. One night, I stopped crying and seduced him. I made love to Jack." If she'd told her parents she had a baby out of wedlock, there would be no home to return to— her little Neon would have been a house on wheels.

"At the time, I didn't think there was another choice if I kept my baby. My little boy needed a father. Soon enough, everything fell into place. We got engaged, I dropped out of school before the spring semester. One day Jack rushed home early from class to tell me the name we should give our unborn child, Hazel. Silently, I prayed for Danny."

All eyes followed her lips, all ears tuned into Wendy's life. "Months later, my water broke, and I gave birth to Hazel. I cried when Danny did not expel from my womb. My little boy died with his daddy. Hazel rejected me as I left her. She refused to suckle from my breasts. Her cries shattered my eardrums when the nurses placed her in my arms for feedings. The feeling of resentment never really disappeared. Of course, I love my daughter, but she was never truly mine; she became Jack's. Only Jack could hold her without tears. Only Jack could chase away nightmares hidden in her room.

—⚋—

A few tiles of the dirt-crusted floor crunched under Hazel's Chuck Taylors as she paced the bathroom from the toilet to the changing table. *I wish I could have come without Dad, but I couldn't be here without him. This isn't something I wanted to write in my following letter, though. But, oh God, I need Mom.* She began to pull the skin away from her knuckles.

How do I tell Mom what happened with Jeremy the other day? How do I tell her that I wasn't ready for him to touch my boobs? Of course, Jeremy is excellent, but am I grown up enough to face the consequences of what we did? Hazel walked over to the toilet. *I might as well pee while I'm in here.* She looked at the undies around her knees, pink with white polka dots—they came a pack of eight others from Wal-Mart. *I'm not even old enough to have panties from fancy stores. I have underwear from a super-center.*

Hazel thought of how her underwear rubbed over the foreign knob in his boxers. Jeremy held her boob over her shirt as he attempted a wet French kiss. Jack was at a meeting he scheduled with Vera, Charlie's Mom. Typically parent-teacher sessions didn't last more than an hour, but Hazel guessed something must have been wrong with Charlie if they needed regular meetings. *The little girl probably started fires or sees dead people.*

Jack came home early. Hazel saw the headlights of the Jeep through her bedroom windows. About the time she looked through the window, a moan escaped Jeremy's lips, and wetness drenched his hunter green plaid boxers.

Her eyes widened as she jumped from Jeremy, threw his pants to him, and pulled her skirt down. "Hurry! My Dad is home! Where are the Language Arts books? We need to look like we were doing homework!" she yelled.

She pulled him up from the bed and pushed him to the floor. "My dad will have a cow if he found out we were both on my bed," she said.

Jeremy didn't say a word as he landed on the floor and opened the book. Footsteps over old wooden stairs creaked as Jack ascended. Hazel pretended to take notes when her Dad opened the door.

"Hey, honey? Whose bike is in the driveway?" Jack looked to the floor as Jeremy bit his lip as he looked from the book to Jack.

"Hi, Mr. Feargus! That's my bike," Jeremy said and gathered up his discarded notebook and English book. "Hazel helped me with our homework for tomorrow's class."

Jack folded his arms and looked at Hazel. Then, he urged, "That's very nice of you to help, but you should have asked before letting him come over."

Hazel sat up and tried to straighten the wrinkles of her crumpled comforter without notice. She raised the pitch in her voice, "I know, Daddy." Hazel emphasized *Daddy* and batted her lashes. She interjected, "but we ran out of time to work on our assignment during lunch. I'm sorry, I will ask the next time."

Jack shrugged his shoulders and smiled. "That's ok, honey," he said and turned his attention to Jeremy. "Dinner will be ready soon, and I think it's probably time for you to go home, Mr. Summers. After that, your family will be wondering where you are."

Jeremy's pants started to fall when he stood on the floor. He dropped his backpack from his shoulder as he caught his jeans. Hazel saw his belt discarded on the floor at the end of her bed, and she hopped Jack didn't see it too. Hazel stopped breathing for a minute as Jeremy's wide eyes begged for help.

"So...so Dad, what's for dinner tonight?" she nervously asked.

Jack pulled his eyes away from the struggling boy. "Probably Hawaiian Pizza," he noted, then laughed as he looked back at the growing red-faced boy. "Son, you need to buy a good belt," Jack jested. Hazel thanked the stars for her father's oblivious nature.

She watched through her window as Jeremy rode his bike down her driveway and off into the streetlights. Her fingers ran over the moist cotton briefs, and she wondered if the wetness was from thier excitement.

Can someone get pregnant by rubbing over clothes? She didn't know. *How do I tell Mom without Dad hearing?* Hazel guessed it was Jack's turn to use the bathroom. She flushed the toilet and exited.

—⚏—

Wendy sat there with Jack in the visiting room. The silence was thick. She couldn't get AA out of her head.

"About eight and a half years later, I discovered wine made me feel like the classy woman sitting at the bar with pearl earrings. The beer gave me the confidence to imagine my life without a husband and daughter, but Jim Beam gave me the ability to turn that confidence into an adventure. In that six-and-a-half-year span, I was three adventures deep when my Subaru t-boned a car. I mean…when I t-boned another car," Wendy said and closed her eyes. She could still hear screaming from the woman in the front seat.

"The crash threw a baby boy from the car seat. The mother survived, but he didn't. I stayed, now I'm here to telling you why I have a prison sentence and mandatory AA meetings every Wednesday.

"Hazel sends me books and writes me letters because she misses me. I never read the books. Why? I couldn't tell ya, but I do her letters. Every day, I call her to find out how her life is on the outside. My daughter finally stopped being a stranger, but this cell block became a sanctuary away from the person I truly resent, Jack," Wendy revealed the dark secrets of her life. The therapy circle grew deathly quiet until the counselor passed the speaking stick onto the next lady.

—⚏—

Jack cleared his throat. Wendy wasn't sure how much time had passed. She stared down at the floor nicer than her cell.

"She's growing up fast. I think she's gotten taller in the last six months," Wendy said.

He turned a little towards his wife and smiled briefly. "Pretty soon, she'll be taller than the boys in her class."

"How did I not notice?" Wendy asked. She still saw Hazel as a child.

Jack bounced his knee and spoke, "How could you? You were too busy counting drinks."

"That's not fair." Wendy's voice rose, "I've always been there. I didn't always understand our daughter, but I was there."

Jack raised his voice, "Remember that Christmas when you drank a fifth of Vlad and fell asleep under the Christmas tree?" He paused and waited for a response. Non came.

"Of course you don't! But our daughter does. Her presents from Santa were drenched in spewed chunks of the lining of your stomach. That was fun telling our eight-year-old mommy had the flu," Jack said.

"I know now that I had a problem," Wendy said.

Losing all composure, Jack spoke, "Too bad you couldn't have figured that out sooner. Not only did you hurt me," Jack stopped and continued, "It doesn't matter that you hurt me. You hurt her. Our little girl," he mumbled over nearby conversations.

"That wasn't my intention," she responded. Wendy held a tight fist in her jumpsuit.

Jack lowered his voice, "If you'd kept your promise, we wouldn't be here."

Wendy spoke louder than a whisper, "That promise to stop drinking ended the day I found out you were fucking one of the moms of your students." She took a deep breath and composed herself.

"I didn't know you knew. That was one time and a decision I sort of fell into." Jack scooched closer and said, "Wendy, when is it my turn to feel loved? You stopped touching me years ago. Why is that?"

Wendy could see her daughter exit the bathroom. *It's time she knew.*

She turned her body to Jack, "You want to know so bad? I wanted to stop before Hazel was even conceived. Hazel isn't your kid!" Then, her voice lowered, "Max was her dad."

All emotion drained from his face. Jack's skin grew grey as he lowered his head into his hands.

Wendy turned to Hazel, "Now you know."

Hazel's face blushed, and her eyes glass. "Mom, what are you saying?" she asked.

If Wendy learned anything from her AA meetings, to be honest with the people around her, you need to be honest with herself. Both pairs

73

of eyes, watery and shocked, stared back at her. Then, for a moment, neither spoke a word.

Addressing her daughter, Wendy spoke, "Honey, it's time you knew. Keeping that secret from you," she cleared her throat, "was more painful than being here. Jack is not your Dad. Your daddy died about fifteen years ago." The words burned in Wendy's mouth. She would have instead sat in solitary, be strip-searched, lose all privileges than to do that again. Wendy drank to forget about the affair. She drank to feel numb because she did love her family. Everything she'd kept a secret unleashed itself into the world. Wendy had nothing left.

Tears ran down Hazel's cheeks as red splotches formed around her lips. Other conversations stopped. Inmates, children, and husbands stopped to watch the drama unfold. Finally, Wendy stood and addressed all those watching, "Get your own lives and leave mine alone."

The female guard who brought Wendy to the visiting area stood behind her with a new handcuffs. "That's enough, Terence. You've lost your visiting privileges."

Jack held Hazel around the shoulders. Both stood like statues, but Jack spoke, "I hope you enjoy the Stephen King books your daughter sent. You're no better than his characters."

"Jack, if this were a King novel, you'd be the drunk, and I'd be leaving the Overlook," Wendy yelled as she walked through the door.

Hazel did not speak most of the way home. No tears, only a blank stare masked her thoughts as she glanced through the windshield. Jack took them through the Dairy Queen drive-thru. "Baby, do you want anything?" he asked. Hazel didn't respond. Jack tried again, "I know it's only Saturday, but it's never too early for a Sunday." He tried to elicit a laugh, but she wouldn't budge.

"Do you want a twist cone?" Jack asked.

She turned her eyes towards him. "No, Jack. I don't want anything," she uttered.

Jack felt his heart stop for only a second. "I don't care what she says! You are my daughter!" he yelled.

"How can I believe either of you? Both of you have lied to me repeatedly. Please, don't talk to me the rest of the night," Hazel pleaded. "I just want to go home." The only voice she wanted to hear was Poppy's.

As requested, Jack drove home in silence with his sad melting ice cream cone and his even sadder daughter. Hazel jumped out of the vehicle when the Jeep parked in the driveway and raced inside the house. The new home Jack and Wendy bought almost a year ago looked grim in the sunset. He pulled out his phone and texted Vera to tell her that he would cancel their date for the night. Jack watched as the sun went down—he wondered if Hazel would ever call him Daddy again.

—⟋⟍—

Hazel fell asleep that night with her sex-ed book tucked beneath the sheets and her phone set to ring.

—⟋⟍—

Wendy walked the cold halls of solitary. "Lupin! You were right!" she screeched.

"Shut it, inmate!" the male guard tightened her cuffs. Then, finally, he pushed her into the cold confinement, unlocked her cuffs, and undid his belt.

Just another day. Wendy thought of the first time Hazel laughed. She smiled at the memory.

Witch Hazel Fixes All

The slam from the storm door against the house Pulled Nev from sleep she'd achieved only an hour before. Everything appeared eerily dark, almost too dark. Nev pulled the cord to her bedside lamp. Nothing.

"Damn. Power's out." Nev opened a drawer in her nightstand and grabbed a flashlight. Her ankles cracked the short walk from her bed to the door. Windblown into the house almost drowned out the chores of Theo's snores.

"Finally asleep," Nev said under her breath.

Nev descended the stairs; each step creaked beneath her weight. She tried to avoid the loose boards as she headed to the first-floor landing. Shadows waltzed from room to room in Nev's peripheral vision. Twice she had to stop herself. *It's nothing.*

Don't look, don't look, don't look; Nev wanted to avoid Saoirse's room. She reached the door to the porch; Nev hesitated, but she pulled the storm door closed. The house grew quieter; she looked over her shoulder to her grandmother's room. Nev gripped her flashlight in a tight grasp. She hadn't been in Saoirse's room since the undertaker pulled the quilted shroud over the body. *She was more than a body.*

Beautiful perfume still filled the space. Through diapers and soiled bed pads, Nev could still smell her grandmother's aroma and matching powder. The dusty bottle sat on the dresser amongst baby pictures of grandkids and the picture of Grandma dancing with Grandpa on their anniversary.

Nev eased herself into the chair next to Saoirse's hospital bed. In the dim light of the flashlight, Nev could make out the indent in the pillow; pieces of Saoirse's hair stuck to the cases. Four days dragged on; four days came and went since the death.

"I promised Mom I would give a speech tomorrow." Nev laid her head in the rails of the bed. "I know what I want to say, but it needs to be written." She allowed tears to stream down.

Nev found a pen and notepad on a try table. She held the flashlight in her mouth as she scribbled down thoughts.

- Grandma's slumber parties
- ~~Winnie the Poo cereal in the morning.~~ No, no one will care about that.
- Playing dress-up—That picture of us tucked away in my drawer. I should mention that.
- ~~Maybe a little humor with the wooden spoon?~~ Hmmm... probably not.
- That time she sang to me under the pine trees. I need to add that.
- My best friend.

Just write the speech!

Thank you all for coming. She would have loved the beautiful flowers and company. We have not gathered to only mourn the loss of Saoirse O'Leary, but we are all the representation of the life she lived. She brought us all into this world. I want to think of her life as a celebration—the lives she touched, the memories we shared, and the importance she placed on each of us.

She was and is my Grandma. I can only recount my memories of her, but I know she loved all of us dearly. So I invite you all to take a moment to close your eyes and think of the light she brought. Think of a time she touched you profoundly, whether in humor, her wit, advice she gave, or the way she listened. Remember her as Grandma, Mom, sister, aunt, or friend. Remember how she was—not the way she died. Remember how she lived.

Grandma was my best friend. She taught me to sew, crotchet, and listen to others. Her hands, beautiful hands held mine as we sat in the car, as she rubbed my back on sleepovers. Those beautiful hands whipped countless tears away. I would never give up that time spent. My favorite picture is of the two of us in front of the pink dollhouse.

I'm wearing a crown, tutu, and tap shoes. She's holding me as we pose for the picture. What wasn't captured on paper and ink was the slumber party we had. What isn't pictured is when we sat under the pine trees while she sang, "You are my Sunshine." I was so fascinated because she loved me enough to compare me to sunshine. Those memories aren't captured on video or pictures, but I keep them here (point to head) and here (point to heart).

I want you all to think about the sunshine, the flowers, even the rainy days. She's here and in all of us—as long as we continue to remember her. Also, remember that witch hazel fixes all. Grandma would want me to remind you all of that.

She was Driving Miss Daisy, and I was her Tinker Bell.

Nev pulled the flashlight from her teeth. *This is the speech for the funeral.* She pulled herself from the chair. Perfume wafted through the room.

"Wish me luck tomorrow, Grandma." Nev left the room and went to bed. The speech stayed tucked against her chest as she slept

Christian Camp for the Non-Believer

Sunday school taught that God created the world in seven days, but it was day seven of Hell for Poppy. She had one day left before the grace of mercy would relieve her of this camp of torture. Every day, the counselors roused the youngsters from their sleep for a light breakfast, morning prayer, and a hike to Bible lessons.

Poppy roused from a sleep that had reached REM only a couple of hours before, inedible food washed down with watery OJ, and a sweaty climb entirely uphill to lessons about heaven out of reach. Poppy felt her punishment from her last report card. Miriam punished her daughter to a seven-day prison sentence at Lamb Christian Camp for Troubled Youth instead of summer school. No books, no phone, and no Hazel.

Poppy looked past overlapping pine trees; at the bottom of the mountain, she could still see Claire Lake. She envisioned herself in a canoe reading a book. Poppy refused to let the thought of jet skiers, pontoon tourists, or screaming swimming children ruin the pleasantries of the lake. However, anywhere was better than Camp Lamb.

Poppy's books of twisted fairytales, read on a comfy couch, were replaced with daily devotions on stiff wooden benches. She was forced out of the comfort zone she filled with sticker books, spy gear, and old plastic play shoes. Those things were replaced by popsicle sticks, modeling clay, and a stern look from the instructor if one did not "play" correctly. Afternoon swimming with the other eight-year-olds turned from Marco Polo into salvation from the devil through baptism—and ghost stories told around the campfire only pertained to the Holy Ghost. Poppy didn't understand why her mother thought it was so urgent now to be saved by Jesus. They'd only been to church a handful of times before. She didn't understand why she had to be sent to camp instead of Sunday School.

In the first couple days of camp, Poppy tried to smile, adjust to the activities, and enjoy the outdoors, but her nerves were worn thin from the ingenuine bliss of the councilors and the unsuspecting campers. Miriam forbade her daughter from swearing, but Poppy couldn't help but comment under her breath, "Why are these people so damn happy all the time?"

—m—

Day 7

"Are you gonna eat your eggs?" a boy with a blonde bowl cut asked. *I didn't know he could speak!*

Poppy pushed her remaining breakfast towards him. "It's all yours," she said and scrunched her nose in disgust. "You like them? I've never tasted scrambled eggs runny and powdery at the same time," Poppy stated with repulsion.

His eyes were downcast as he answered, "They're ok; it beats not eating anything for breakfast."

Poppy continued the conversation. "Doesn't your mom make you food in the morning?" she asked and sipped her glass of OJ. "Or is she the mom that hands out soggy cereal for breakfast?"

"I get food when she has time." The boy shoved a spoon full of drippy eggs in his mouth. Poppy gagged.

A camp counselor stood and blew her whistle. The dining hall progressively quieted down. "Good morning, campers! We're doing something a little different today. Instead of your regular scheduled Bible lessons, we will be splitting you up into groups based on your tables to attend different activities for your last day," she exclaimed and pointed to Poppy's table. "This group will be attending The Dirt of Our Sins." She continued down the rows of tables with other activities such as, Reach for the Heavens (Rockwall Climbing) and Almost Stoning of Mary Magdalen (Dodge Ball).

Poppy raised her hand. "Excuse me, but what is The Dirt of Our Sins?" she asked.

"Oh honey, It's a blast! It's a new activity we created where we can fling our sins away. You'll have fun!" The councilor lightly squeezed Poppy's right hand and continued speaking to the groups. "Alright, everyone, let's head out," the counselor said and dismissed the groups.

—⁊ℕ⁊—

The campers in Poppy's group hiked the downward spiral of rocks, dirt clots, and exposed tree roots. They descended the ravine filled with swamp area and mud; overcast light broke through heavy branches and pine needles, but Poppy held her nose away from the smell of rotting Earth breaking the barricade of her nostrils, while avoiding a fall that would break an arm or neck.

Counselor Christy held a fist in the air. Then, she called to the group, "We've arrived at the lowest point of Camp Lamb."

Poppy whispered to Bowl Cut Boy, "More like Camp Lame, right?" She laughed—he looked through her with a vague expression.

"Alright, kids, it's time to get dirty with your sins as you chuck them away! It would be best if you took your shoes off, so you are fully in touch with Earth." Christy blew her whistle to commence *fun.*

Bowl Cut Boy and others removed socks, shoes, shirts and dove into the dark sludge without a second thought. Poppy bent over to look at her shoes on the bank of land as she slowly untied them. *Maybe if I untie them slow enough, I won't have to get in.*

Christy walked over towards her and asked, "Are you getting in?"

Poppy glanced up and hesitated before she spoke, "I don't know… Is this mud sanitary? It looks questionable to me."

"Of course, it's not," Christy laughed. "The unspoken sins of hundreds dwell down here. Only from the light through those trees do we emerge from our confessions."

"Whatever," Poppy said under her breath and rolled her eyes. She unlaced her shoes as she stepped into the cold enveloping suction of ick around her legs. A boy not far threw mud directly in her face. Poppy heard his laughter when the clump of muck rolled down her forehead and over her lips. Violent shivers rocked her body when crud leaked into her mouth. Rubbing mud away from her eyes clouded her eyesight and caked blonde lashes. Poppy imagined the creepy crawlers living in the filth and then visualized them infesting her blond French braids. She screamed as her eager hands scrubbed the dirt from her head and body; tears mixed with mud in streams down her face.

Blindly, Poppy reached down to grab a fist full of sludge and rocks from the swamp. She whispered her sin, "I snuck M&M's from home to eat in my bunk." Poppy released the heavy concoction from her fingertips.

A thud not far from her landed in the mud amongst the screams of Counselor Christy and the other children. She wiped away the remaining dried dirt crusting around her eyes.

Bowl Cut Boy lay in a heap with blood oozing from the mud on his head.

"Is Bowl Cut Boy's mom coming to get him early?" Poppy asked Counselor Christy.

"Unfortunately, Camp Lamb was Adam's purgatory between foster homes. We don't know where he's going."

"Oh...I thought he had family...When will the rest of us get to leave tomorrow?" Poppy asked.

The wide grin and sparkling eyes on Chrisy's face all week disappeared. "The children will be released with their parents around noon," she stated.

Poppy grinned. "Good! I miss my Mom soooooo much!" she exclaimed and turned away.

Counselor Christy Grabbed Poppy's arm. "We've spoken with your mother after the incident, and we all feel that another week at Camp lamb would do you right. I don't believe you've accepted the salvation of our Lord," Christy almost snickered. Poppy nearly collapsed. "Tomorrow, we will be assigning you to a new cabin. You will learn to walk with the rest of God's Children."

Please Lord, please let me leave. I promise to do better in school. I promise to listen to my mother when she is speaking. Please. I promise not to eat M&M's in my bunk. Don't leave me here!

Upon the Vanity

Jack parked the Jeep in the driveway but hesitated to shut off the ignition. His gaze lingered. Hazel abruptly exited and slammed the door to the car, ran upstairs to her room, and dropped to the indigo bean bag chair. The beating of breath became shallow as shadows stretched into elongated blots of ink. Late afternoon sun dropped below the horizon of Hazel's window frame. She sat in the darkened corner of her bedroom and watched as streetlights became her night light. Sweat collected around her upper lip, salt from dry streaked tears crusted the skin she thoroughly moisturized that morning.

Heat pooled through the enclosed space. A feeling of claustrophobia surrounded her, but Hazel wanted to feel the suffering warmth. At least she was feeling something. After visiting with her Mom in the woman's prison, discovering Jack's affair, and Wendy's betrayal, Hazel wanted silence. She wanted the voices of her parents and their words of infidelity to stop echoing in her ears. The day was almost done, but the next day would not be any easier. At some point, twenty-four hours from then, she would have to interact with Jack. He would console her, tell her she would always be his daughter, and then apologize for *his* recent affairs.

Hazel stood from the chair that stuck to her sweaty back when she stood. Her breath felt heavy in her chest as she set the A/C to sixty-three degrees. Sweaty jean fiber clung to her belly and legs. Like a second skin, Hazel peeled her jeans off. The motion of undressing and throwing sweaty garments to the hardwood floor was recorded by the mimicked images reflecting in the vanity mirror. Hazel stopped to glance at the face looking back—she looked like her mother. She looked like a young Wendy—the way red hair curled around her naked shoulders and the edges of her teal bra. Hazel stared at the pouch over her abs that made her neither thin nor obese and the freckles that covered lengthy her bare body. She sat at the upholstered faded green wooden bench to not look at herself but to see her mother. Hazel didn't want to picture her mother in that jumpsuit—she didn't want to think of the way they left Wendy.

—⚅—

"Come here, honey," Wendy coaxed little Hazel over to the vanity. "You can sit with Mommy while she does her makeup."

Hazel sat at the edge of the bench. Her eyes wandered over the wood, pealing green painted, makeup-stained desk. Her fingers brushed over the chipped pink and purple flowers hand-designed by Wendy. Amongst hundreds of brushes, makeup lay in no order at the base of the mirror. Splattered and speckled, Hazel wondered how Wendy could see her reflection. Intermixed with used brushes were lipsticks in shades of red, purple, gold, pallets of eyeshadows depicted in every color, and a particular plastic container of rouge lay at Hazel's reach.

"Can you stay with me tonight? Rub my back until I go to sleep?" Hazel asked as she raised her eyes to meet Wendy's in the mirror. A second later, Wendy flicked makeup from her brush and rolled her eyes. Then, she set down her tools of disguise and turned towards her daughter. The bench creaked and wobbled with the shifting with any slight movement.

"I love you, but you know that's not possible. As I've told you many times before, I need these nights away from this house, away from Daddy," Wendy declared, then picked up a thick bristled brush and swirled it in pink rouge. She dotted her daughter's nose in pink. "Baby, I need this to stay sane. I pray to God you will never have to understand," Wendy whispered.

"Understand what?" Hazel asked. She looked from her mother to the uncapped lipstick ready to be twisted and exposed.

"It's nothing," Wendy hesitated, "nothing. But, little lady, I think it's time for you to get upstairs before Jack realizes I let you stay up."

Hazel stood from the seat and said, "Mommy, I want to stay up with you." She hugged her mother around the shoulders from behind.

Wendy's purple nails held her daughter's petite arms. "I'm finished with my makeup, and I'll be leaving in a few minutes," Wendy sighed. In that brief moment, Hazel studied the small wrinkles forming around her mother's rose-red lips, highlighted heat in Wendy's cheeks from blush and mascara that coated drama to the deep green of Wendy's eyes. Hazel wanted to look like her mother when she grew up.

The observation found in the warm glow of the makeup mirror was interrupted with Jack's throat clearing, "Miss Hazel, don't you think it's a little late for you to be awake?"

Wendy let go, and Hazel responded, "Yes, Daddy."

"To bed or the tooth fairy will pass you by tonight," Jack ushered his daughter to bed.

The last Hazel remembered was red curly hair draped over bare shoulders and the edges of a black lace bra as her parents started the tenth argument of the day.

—ᵚ—

Tears formed in the eyes Hazel shared with her mother as she glanced through the same mirror ten years later. The chill from the A/C stung her skin. In utter disbelief from the visit, Hazel didn't know what to do next. She wanted to curl up on the bed with her highly worn-out baby blanket as her mother rubbed her back. Never again. Hazel could no longer smell her mother's perfume waft past her bedroom. Jack and Wendy had the final fight; Hazel heard only silence. Wendy was gone, and Hazel could feel her absence.

Wanna See Something Cool?

He shouldn't have listened to her. His damned cousin. That Christmas when cousin Amber invited Danny into her bedroom to see something remarkable. Danny knew that he should have told his parents about the gerbil—he knew that he should have told his parents about the man that could smell his fear, but he didn't.

—◊◊—

"Danny," Doctor Theo interrupted his thoughts as she looked over her scribbled notes. "Tell me about that Christmas fourteen years ago. Can you tell me about the incident?"

Danny closed his eyes. His breathing caught in his chest. "It's silly. I never told anyone because of the superstition of the situation. As an adult, I know that I will be fine, but I still worry that he will find me," Danny revealed.

"Who, Danny? Who will come for you?" Doctor Theo leaned forward.

He whispered, "The creeper."

—◊◊—

Snow dusted the yard, and a red door was garnished with Christmas lights. Through frosted windows, a statue of Santa Claus stood by the house entrance amongst other decorations of red and green. Danny's parents dragged him for a visit with family they typically only saw once a year. Danny stood bundled in a coat with his hand in his mother's while she rang the doorbell. A moment that lasted centuries in the freezing wind, chattering teeth, frostbitten toes, Aunt Joanne opened the door.

Amber stood at the foot of the steps. She welcomed the family and invited Danny upstairs; he followed. She was significantly older with significantly longer legs. His little feet practically ran to keep up with her as they raced up the tan carpeted stairs. Long dark hair flipped over her shoulder as she stepped in front of her bedroom.

Amber turned and put her hand out, pushing Danny back. "Wait here. I need to put some stuff back into my magic box," she said, then grew close to his face. He could feel her breath on his face as she spoke, "Do you know what weed is?"

He shook his head and answered, "Is it like grass outside?"

Amber laughed, stepped inside, and shut the door close to his face. Patiently, Danny waited.

Through the white paneled door, she yelled, "You can come in now."

A haze filled the room. Then, finally, movement in Danny's peripheral vision caught his attention. Small creatures with brown and white fur scurried around a green plastic wheel. "What are those things?" Danny inquired.

Her fingers hooked on the cage as she shook it enough to knock the animal off the wheel. She noted, "Gerbils. They're kind of like mice." Amber's eyes poured over Danny as he reached out towards the minuscule beings.

"Do they have names?" Danny asked. Cold metal grazed his fingers when Danny stuck them between the purple metal wire cage to touch the fur.

"I don't name things that won't live long enough to know their name," she continued. "Do you wanna see something cool?"

The boy nodded in response. Ashley took a gerbil out of the cage as the creature squealed and tried to pull away.

"Follow me," she ushered Danny out the door.

In compliance, Danny followed her back down the stairs and to the kitchen. It was adjacent to the stairwell and the isolated sitting room. Faintly, he could hear the adults laughing in the dining room. Easily, Danny imagined himself a mouse lost in the maze of this house. The first floor remained significantly warmer as they stood in the glow of the kitchen. Amber looked frantic as she wandered around the cooking space opening draws, looking for something.

"Hold your hand out," she said.

More squeaking sounded as she placed the gerbil in his hands. The white fur felt soft under the pads of his little fingers. The nameless gerbil trembled in Danny's palm as he held it close to his face. Dark lentil eyes wondered rapidly over his features.

Amber turned towards the boy with an expression of menace masking her eyes and upturned mouth. They stood opposite one other at the island. His nose just barely reached the countertop. An object was held tucked behind her back when she stepped closer. "Hold the rodent onto the counter. Don't let go, and make sure to keep his tail out," Amber commanded.

Rough wood scraped his elbows as he reached for the island. Danny and the rodent locked each other in direct eye contact. "Why do I have to keep his tail out?" he asked. Danny pulled the animal close to his chest.

"You'll see," she said.

A wince escaped Danny's mouth when he grazed his skin over the unfinished wooden countertop. The object from her back was revealed when metal glittered across the sleek sharpness of the knife. She held it high and slashed it across the tail. Danny screamed as the animal shook violently in a panic to escape his trembling hands. Tears formed in his eyes when Danny released the squirming creature from his loose grasp. The creature slipped away in a mess of trailing blood off the counter and to the floor. Legs trembled as he cracked his knees against the tile next to the gerbil. Its head turned at an awkward angle, and the belly no longer expanded with air filling its body. Danny's fingers stretched out to the white fur coated in the gore pooling around the wounded tail; red painted the tips of his fingers. Scraped knees and paper cuts were nothing compared to that of fresh crimson coating the floor. Danny had never seen a dead animal that closes before. He had never seen anything bleed out before.

Amber snatched Danny's arm and brought him to his feet. Her face reddened from anger. "I told you not to let him go! So now he's dead!" she yelled. Her face was close to his. "You killed him," she said, slapping her hand across the arm she held tightly. "Go upstairs and think about what you did."

Danny could only whimper. The tension in her hardened grip released as she let go of his limp arm. "When you come back downstairs, we are going to watch a movie," Amber said.

His chin quivered, and pain reverberated across the tension in his forehead. Salty droplets blinded Danny's vision as he stumbled up the stairs. The door glided across the carpet when he turned the knob and face planted to the tan carpet. Soft fibers of Amber's rug soaked up drool and tears. Danny's head turned over his left shoulder to see the left-over gerbils racing around the squeaking wheel. They carried on as though nothing was amiss. *But, if I tell, will she cut off my toes?*

Danny slipped back into the kitchen. Screaming for his parents would have been too obvious, and Amber would have discovered him before he reached safety. Blood no longer coated the floor, and the dead body no longer lay limp. Amber worked fast; he'd only been upstairs a few minutes. Fresh lemon cleaner masked the smell of pine tree Christmas candles in the next room. His feet slipped onto the wet floor as his rear connected with the solid floor; the fall echoed around the kitchen. Heavy footsteps vibrated the floors under Danny's butt. Amber ran to the kitchen and snatched Danny up by the arm. Her touch was like fire; he wanted to pull away the second her fingers wrapped around the tenderness of his bicep. She was the authority, and he was the child.

"What took you so long, squirt? Were you rooting around in my shit?" she asked and patted Danny's pockets. "I was only going to make you watch the first movie, but now you get to watch them both."

The tv room already filled the silence with screaming people when she sat him down on the couch. "If you tell anyone about anything that happened tonight, the man in the movie will come for you," she snickered.

Danny held his breath and tried to force the tears away, but her imposing presents made it difficult. Amber was the hardened grip that nailed him to the island, and he was the gerbil about to leap to suicide.

Amber slapped her fingers across his arm when a tear rolled down his cheek. "You have to stop crying. If someone sees, I'll tell my Mom you killed my pet. Then, I'll tell the Creeper to follow you home. You don't want that do you?" She grabbed his chin.

Danny pulled away from her gripped fingers. "I won't say anything."

Slowly, he moved to the opposite side of the couch. A winged creature flew across the screen, eating up the lives of people from cars and buses. The creature carried himself like a man hidden within cornfields and an abandoned church. People begged for their lives as he used his talons and homemade weapons for ripping away the flesh of victims. This was the Creeper Amber threatened him with. As the victims lost the vicious game of tag, Danny saw their death. He saw what would happen if he spilled the events of that Christmas to his parents.

—⟊—

Doctor Theo stopped writing moments before. "Why didn't you say anything?" she asked.

"I honestly thought that thing would come for me," Danny mumbled and rubbed his temples. "There are ancient origin stories of superstitions beginning. I never realized some superstitions could originate from a family Christmas."

"Do you still worry that he may come for you?" she asked held the pen erect. "Does this...creature...scare you now that you've told me?"

"Yes." Danny leaned back in his seat and closed his eyes.

"What happened after the movies were over?" Theo questioned.

—⟊—

The creature feature ended before dinner. Aromas of ham, mashed potatoes, and corn buried themselves under Danny's nose. Amber led him by the hand to the dining room decorated with a Christmas tree in the corner and the nativity scene placed upon a white lace doily on the table. His tears were dry. Danny's mother asked what they were doing before dinner—she didn't hear a peep. He was screaming in his head, *tell her! Tell her about the gerbil. Tell her about the Creeper.* A kick from across the table connected with Danny's shin. Amber's eyes met his; he remembered the man would come if he told. Instead, Danny scraped the fork across his uneaten food and lied, "We watched some Christmas movies." his eyes remained on the glaring eyes of Baby Jesus and the Virgin Mary. Lying was bad.

A Moment

Mavis shook the Magic 8 Ball and asked, "Is it the right time to leave?"

Through the haze of blue, she saw the answer, "Signs point to yes."

One hundred ninety days until the ceremony, rings, and the bouquet toss, Mavis packed a duffle bag with the few things she needed.

Among a stack of movies, she left a note with her ring saying, "I may be back, but I don't know when."

Mavis left before Joe came home for their usual movie nights, Chinese take-out, and cuddling above the clothes. Cold feet didn't describe her feeling for marriage; stifling, clammy, a wet sock sort of feeling would envelop her if she stayed one more night.

—⚏—

"Do I stay in this direction?" Mavis asked.

The Magic 8 Ball responded, "It is decidedly so."

Trees with budded leaves and dead grass passed Mavis in hundreds along the highway. Stray aqua blue strands lose from her limp braided hair twirled through the whoosh of air circulating through open windows of the beat-up orange VW Bug. Mavis figured Joe called her cell at least a hundred times—by now, he would have heard her phone ringing from the hamper. Buried beneath a pile of dirty clothes she planned to wash the next day. Mavis cut off any communication with him and anyone who knew her.

Every cop in chase rearing her bumper left an anxious, excited feeling until they maneuvered around her bug. Not that she was ready to go back, but Mavis kind of hoped someone was looking for her. Blurred twigs, desolate fields not yet planted spread for miles in a colorless scab of land.

"Why didn't I head for a warmer climate?" she asked no one.

Mavis blasted Portishead through the speakers. The bass vibrated in irregular beats against her shins as the lead voice, smooth in tone, took a bite of her soul. Hyper focused on the road and singing; her mind drew hypnotized by the never-ending cycle of broken white lines on the highway. She thought of Joe.

Joe's glasses reflected the shallow glow of his computer screen. Mavis crawled up the foot of the bed and intervened herself between Joe and his work. He tilted his head slightly into the indent of his backrest as she combed through chest hair. A small exhale of breath escaped him when her hands traveled south of his pectorals. Mavis kissed Joe's dry lips and trailed her fingers to the edge of his bunny trail before he pushed her hands away from his exposed belly.

"Honey. I'm not in the mood," Joe sighed.

"Did I do something wrong?" she asked. Then, widened eyes and confused, she said, "You were in the mood a second ago."

"Please, not tonight? I still have a ton of filing and complaint write-ups to get done before I can deal with tomorrow's new set of complaints coming through the welfare office," he replied.

"Can you at least touch me with a little affection?" She bit her lip and said, "Like you used to? The way you used to cuddle me and do work at the same time?"

He gave no notice to her.

She asked, "Do you remember when we would put on movies…if you had work to bring home, I would sprawl out on our bed, and you would put the Mac on my butt?"

"Yeah, I remember," Joe assured Mavis and continued to type.

Mavis tried again, "Every time you said that cheesy line about being at the butt of your job."

"Yup," he responded

Mavis sat cross-legged and voiced, "Yoo-hoo?" Then, she moved the laptop away from his line of vision.

"Please. I can't entertain you right now. There is so much that needs to be done. I love you, but honey, there is not enough time between now and time for work for me to finish filing, writing up these analyses', and touch you with affection," Joe replied, then grabbed his computer.

Mavis got out of bed, turned the lights off, then buried herself amongst the comforter on her side of the bed. Finally, she simply said, "Night."

"Goodnight. I love you," Joe said and leaned in to kiss her, but she flipped to the other side.

"You don't have time," Mavis muttered.

—𝔪—

Headlights shimmied over the chipped painted sign welcoming Mavis to the Village of Claire Lake. A flash from the red gas light lit up the dashboard.

I just filled you up! At a creep speed, Mavis drove until she saw a lonely gas station not far from a dark body of water in the distance. Dim lights in the convenience store showed closure, but a dull yellow glow exhumed the cracked and aged parking lot.

Coldness crept up her boots as her feet touched the cement. Goosebumps stung her skin inside the thick cable-knit sweater encasing her body. *Only one pump. Odd.* She unhinged the gas cap and placed the nozzle inside.

This town was old but not decrepit. The wind began to whip off the lake; she could see this place thrive during the summer. Boats spread on warm waves, children's sand creations on the beaches, and families camping under clear skies. Few buildings lined the street—Katie's Ice Cream & Candies, Harmon's Bait and Tackle, Jacob's Bar and Diner, and… a man lying in the middle of traffic! Mavis dropped the handle and ran to the man in the middle of the road.

"Sir! Do you need help?" Mavis asked, then searched her pockets and remembered she left her phone at the apartment.

"Damn," she said to herself. "I can't call for help, but I can take you to the nearest hospital."

The man sat up on his elbows and turned his head slightly towards her. "New here, huh?" he inquired.

She slowed her pace and said, "You could be killed! Someone could drive through here and run you flat."

He lay back down. "Eh, I've been hurt worse."

Mavis looked back towards her car. "Ok then, I need to go...pay for gas."

"Just slip your money through the mail slot in the convenience store's door. Ed'll get it in the morning," he offered, then continued to stare at the changing streetlights. "He never stays past ten."

"Thanks," Mavis said; she crossed her arms and held them close to her body. "Is there something I can do for you?"

"Mmmm...Nope," the man said without urgency.

Mavis wanted to leave this person, mind her business, but she couldn't stop rubbernecking at the human wreck lying on the ground. "Can you tell me your name?" she asked.

He rolled his head to look at her. "That all depends. Are you just passing through?"

"There's no plan to stay," Mavis assured.

"You running away from something?" he asked.

"Sort of a someone. Sort of a commitment," Mavis said and shrugged.

"Do you need to be taken somewhere?" he asked.

"NO!" she answered too quickly. "No, no. I'm fine."

"Probably good, my Subaru runs like shit," he said and turned away.

"I'm not sure how to continue with plans." Her toes wiggled in her boots to bring back warmth as she stood there.

"You don't have to tell me more. I get it." He stuck his hand out to shake hers. "My name's Frank. I'll tell you my name," he mused.

"What if I do stay?" she asked and shook his hand.

"Then you have nothing else going for ya in life. People don't tend to just pass through Claire Lake. Unless it's busy season." He took a moment to look her over then asked, "Now, what's your name?"

"Mavis. Mavis Doubtfire."

"Like the movie?" Frank asked.

"Something like that," Mavis laughed and began to walk away.

His voice rang through the dark, "Gossip rushes through this town faster than money in my pocket at the bar." Frank stood up and warned, "Careful, by morning someone'll have seen your car, and by afternoon there'll be stories passed from person to person saying you are friend or foe." He arched his back and cracked it. "Do you need a place to stay the night?" he asked.

"Wouldn't that invoke gossip if I went home with you?" she jested.

"Oh Hell yes," Frank laughed and continued, "I didn't mean with me. My friend Corrine runs our local hotel. It's not much, but there's a history that stretches over...I think...a hundred and fifty years."

"Is this a tourist trap?" Mavis asked.

"No, this is my way of getting rid of you so I can continue with my peaceful evening," he said.

"Thanks, Frank," she said as she walked towards her car.

"No problem, ma'am. If you go straight, right before you hit the lake, there will be a road on the left. Follow that a little way. It leads to a dead end. The Hotel Claire will be there; you can't miss it."

"Sounds easy enough," she said, then yelled, "Try not to get hit."

Frank waved her on. "If you stay too long in this town, you'll never leave," he warned.

—m—

The road was closed in by thick woods to the left, and hints of the lake gapped between trees older than the settlement of Claire Lake. Mavis could see an imposing building nestled amongst forestry near the end of the road with two old-fashioned streetlamps leading to the loose gravel driveway. The lamp lights flickered and danced within the glass walls. The closer she drove to the Hotel Claire, the clearer she could see the tattered white wood paneling, windows with swirled glass designs framed in black, and more lamp lights wavered near the entrance. Finally, Mavis parked her bug and grabbed the Magic 8 Ball.

"Am I safe here?" She shook the ball in her hands.

"Reply hazy, try again," the Magic 8 Ball answered.

Mavis shook it harder, "Should I stay here?"

"Yes," bobbed to the top.

Alright then. Mavis threw the ball into the bag in her front seat. She rushed out of the cold to the hotel door. *Melted burning candles lit the lamps. Curious.*

A woman with dull dyed dark hair sat at the desk with glasses near the tip of her nose and a book in hand. A romance novel—the cover displayed a woman barely covered by a satin robe draped over the lap of a floppy-haired muscular man on a horse.

"I would like a room," Mavis said.

"One second, Sugar. I'm almost done with this page." The woman bit her lip as her eyes darted from line to line. Then, finally, she dog eared the page and placed her gold-framed glasses on the counter, and said, "Sorry, I can't get enough of these romances. They're so unrealistic, but a girl can dream, right?"

"Exactly! Sometimes we just need to figure out what those dreams are," Mavis said; she smiled and sat her duffel at her feet.

"What kind of room are you looking for?" the woman asked; she slid over the registry book and placed her glasses back on.

"I have no preference. I'm just going to be here for the night," Mavis said.

"Then we might as well welcome you to our little town with some luxury." She squinted her eyes and asked, "You're new here, right?"

Mavis nodded and said, "Yes. I just drove into town."

"I can tell," the woman guessed. But, then, she looked Mavis up and down, "You look like a breath of fresh air."

"It's nice to stick out," Mavis said. "How about a room that looks over the lake and a queen-sized bed?" she asked, then clicked her pen.

Mavis nodded, "That works for me."

The décor lining the room from floor to ceiling caught Mavis' attention. Floral carpets embossed with hues of pink and brown, golden lamps with pearl beaded shades, old but preserved books covered the shelves on the far wall, chairs, and couches upholstered with yellowing white silk floral prints, and a wooden coffee table closely resembled the one in her grandma's.

"That will be forty-seven even for the night," the woman said.

"Hotel Claire certainly holds a very... antique esthetic," Mavis noted, turned towards the hotel entrance, "I noticed the candle-lit lamps outside."

"Love the glow and mystical feel, but I hate lighting them alone." The lady giggled, "My friend Frank tells me that one of these nights I'm going to be eaten by a bear, a skinwalker, or some shit like that."

"Are you Corrine?" Mavis asked.

"I assume you found Frank laying in the road," Corrine guessed. She stuck her hand out to shake. "Nice to meet ya. You must have made an impression on him...he doesn't talk to anyone."

"No, I just didn't run him over," Mavis laughed. She pulled her wallet from her bag. "I don't mean to be rude, but why does he lay in the road?"

"Frank O'Hara is an odd duck. To describe half the things that man does would involve spiked coffee and unmeasurable time," Corrine said and continued, "I just let him go. Frank doesn't ask for much in our friendship."

"He certainly seemed like the type who enjoys alone time. He recommended Hotel Claire to get rid of me." Mavis untangled a wad of twenties and her ID from discarded receipts stuffed in the Coach Wristlet.

"He said that I looked like I needed a place to stay for the night," Mavis said.

Corrine placed her pen over the registry book. "Your money is no good here."

Mavis bit her lip and said, "Oh sorry, do you need a credit card?"

"What I mean is...I know the look you have. But, sometimes a girl just needs a moment," Corrine said.

Mavis nudged the money back into place. "I can't deny that."

Corrine scribbled more into the page. "All that is needed now is a signature. You can use your real name or a fake one. My boss just needs to see that someone signed off."

Pen in hand, Mavis signed, Victoria Winters.

Corrine grabbed a tarnished key with a gold-plated tag. "Room 304 is yours. Sleep well, Vicki."

—ɯ—

"Has Joe noticed I'm gone?" Mavis asked and shook the ball.

The Magic 8 Ball answered simply, "No."

The Orange duffel bag dropped in the middle of the queen-sized bed was the only time marker in the room to represent the year 2020. From the exterior of Hotel Claire to the lobby and in-room 304, this place was stuck in an isolated time. Not that Mavis cared, she loved vintage—she loved that the owner didn't replace the 1800's nostalgia with flat-screen TVs, promotional posters, and modern sculptures.

Mavis scrounged around her bag for a pair of shorts and an oversized t-shirt. But, instead, she found one of Joe's old college shirts mixed in with hers. In a split second, she ripped it out of her bag and threw it to the end of the bed. In a crimson heap, it lay crumpled; she lay outstretched over the comforter and brought Joe's shirt to her chest. Mavis could smell his cologne; she wanted to cry out of confusion for commitment, the love she shared with Joe, and her fear of the future she may have destroyed by leaving. But, stuck mentally in place with a soupy fog blocking any insight into the future—she didn't know how to continue.

A light knock on the door brought Mavis back to the present. The knock came again with a voice, "Corrine sent me to bring towels."

Mavis pulled herself together and tucked the shirt under a pillow. She glanced in the bathroom to find that there were none. "Yes. Thank you!" she said, then opened the door to find a woman dressed in a long blue cotton nightgown with soft white lace.

"It's not exactly a maid's outfit. I live in the hotel," she said.

Mavis noticed that her features were young and untouched by age. "I didn't mean to stare...sorry if I offended you," Mavis said.

"No offense taken! I help Corrine when I can." She handed Mavis the stark white towels and began to walk away.

"Thank you. I guess I was too occupied to notice I had none," Mavis said and continued, "I don't suppose you would know where I could get a cup of tea, do you?"

The nightgown swished around the woman's feet as she turned back to Mavis. "If you wouldn't be opposed to a company, I have French Vanilla Chia and Irish Afternoon in my room."

"That sounds lovely." Mavis grabbed her room key and followed.

—⁊⁊⁊—

"Each room carries its personality, doesn't it?" Mavis said. The women sat in the matching pink upholstered armchairs.

"Indeed, each room was hand-designed years ago," the woman spoke softly.

"Centuries ago." Mavis sipped her tea and said, "I didn't catch your name."

"Oh, how inappropriate of me." The kindness of her face extended to her outreached palm. She said, "My name is Kathleen. Your name on the registry book was Victoria." She tapped her finger on her cup. "I don't mean to be rude, but you don't look like a Victoria."

Mavis lightly shook the woman's hand and replied, "Mavis." A cold zap ignited the webbed nerves in Mavis' hand. Kathleen folded her arm into her lap and wrapped her unblemished and delicate fingers around the teacup.

"Beautiful name. Much more interesting than the name registered," Kathleen said, her eyes held Mavis in place.

"I'm trying to stay hidden," Mavis said.

Mavis wondered if there was an open window somewhere. Cool air snaked around Mavis' limbs. "It's a bit chilly in here. Can I grab you a blanket?" Mavis asked.

"No, my dear. I'm quite alright." Kathleen sipped her tea and continued, "I never feel the chill."

Mavis frowned. *God, I wish I didn't get cold.* "As long as you're sure," Mavis said.

She couldn't help her hyper-focus on the cup in Mavis' hand. A teacup with swirls and stars. Her brain started to feel fuzzy; her vision focused then panned out in blurs. Mavis rubbed the mascara from her eyes. *I'm just tired from the drive.*

Kathleen poured more tea into her cup. "I am interested in what brings you here."

"I'm not sure." Mavis cleared her throat and continued, "My gas light came on, and I had to stop."

"What brought you on this journey?" Kathleen asked.

"My Magic 8 Ball and a search for answers," Mavis said as she stared into her cup. She could almost read her tea leaves. The porcelain felt heavy in her hands.

"I think you do know what you want." Kathleen took a sip and said, "I think you know the answers to your questions."

There was a long pause. Swallowing and deep breaths overwhelmed Mavis. Kathleen's voice became distant, but Mavis watched the swirls in her cup twirl. Images from the morning struck Mavis. She saw herself leave the apartment, her ring on the coffee table, a bag full of meaningless items. A headache stretched over her brows at the thought. She left Joe. Swirled visions of her day twirled into blurred dance around the room. Mavis couldn't catch her breath.

Kathleen's cool hand reached for the girl sitting across from her. "Mavis, what are you afraid of?"

"I...I don't know. I don't know what's happening?" Mavis dropped to her knees and her tea to the carpet. She couldn't help but stare at the cup. "Did you put something in my tea?" Mavis whispered.

"No." Kathleen sat on the floor next to Mavis. She brought her hand to the girl's back and said, "That would hurt the baby."

Then all was quiet. All movement stopped. For a moment, Mavis felt nothing; she saw nothing. The pounding in her ears paused. Mavis floated in the space behind her eyes; she blinked away the cloud blurring her vision. Then all she saw was Kathleen.

"What did you say?" Mavis asked. "How did you know?"

Kathleen helped Mavis from the floor. She placed the girl back in the chair and said, "I was never blessed with a child, but I can always tell when a woman is expecting." Kathleen pulled a soft pink robe around her shoulders.

Once again, Kathleen asked, "What are you afraid of?"

Mavis closed her eyes and held her arms close to her body. "I'm afraid to be too comfortable with one person. You see, the people closest are the ones to hurt you the deepest. Not that I believe Joe would hurt me, but I fear that I am the wrecking ball." Mavis looked back into her cup. Clear. No swirls.

Kathleen scooted her chair closer to Mavis. Jasmine perfume lingered in the space they shared. "You can't be afraid of the future. If you fear for something that has yet to come, nothing will be accomplished. Think about the moment. The one we are currently living," Kathleen said. Her chilled hand touched Mavis' belly. "Think about her. Be strong for her."

"What if I've already pushed away that life with Joe by being here?" Mavis asked.

"Call him. Tell him what he needs to know," Kathleen said.

—⚭—

"Does Joe miss me?" Mavis asked.

"Better not tell you now." The Magic 8 Ball responded.

The phone rang twice. "Hello! Did you find her?" Joe practically shouted.

"Joe, she's been found," Mavis said.

"OH MY GOD! Baby! I didn't recognize the number. Where are you? Are you ok? Do you want me to come to get you? Do you still need some time? I'm so sorry. Will you say something?" Joe was frantic.

"Take a breath. In and out." Mavis paused, "Maybe even a couple more breaths for good measure." She, too, took a long breath and continued, "I'm fine. More than a little overwhelmed. Joe, I'm scared."

"Mavis, I'm scared too." His frazzled words grew heavy over the phone, "I know that lately, I haven't been extremely present. But, Mavis, I am so sorry," Joe said.

"I don't want to say that I haven't felt left out, but it's more than that." Finally, Mavis gathered her thoughts and said, "I'm scared to lose you, but I'm scared of losing the both of you."

"Both of us?" Joe asked.

"Yeah, both of you." Mavis lowered her voice, "My period's been late for the last two months." She took a breath before speaking, "I thought maybe it was just stress from the wedding…I wasn't sure until last week."

Joe remained silent on his end.

Mavis spoke, "Joe?"

"I'm here," he said. "Just digesting. Why didn't you tell me?"

"We aren't ready, but I needed a moment to think about what I even wanted," Mavis said.

"Did you think that I would be mad?" Joe asked.

"I didn't know how you would react," Mavis said.

"Mavis! I'm coming. I'm coming to you and the baby." A crash came to his end, and Mavis winced. He came back on the line. "Sorry, I dropped my phone." Joe's voice softened, "Sweetie, tell me where you are. I need to see you."

—⟳—

"Will Joe be here soon?" Mavis asked the Magic 8 Ball.

"Cannot predict now." The Magic 8 Ball responded. Mavis threw the ball to the head of her bed and went to the lobby.

"Well, don't you look fresh this morning?" Corrine said.

"I feel much better! My fiancé is meeting me here later today," Mavis said. She pulled out her card. "I think I'm going to need a few more days."

"I'll give you a fantastic rate!" Corrine pulled a calculator up on her phone.

"Thank you for sending up towels last night," Mavis smiled.

Corrine stopped typing and looked up. "I didn't send towels."

"Oh…then Kathleen must have known I needed them. I'm glad she did. She helped me decide what I needed to do."

A sigh and a deep breath brought Corrine from around the desk. "I should have known. Damn. I should have known?"

Mavis scrunched her brows and said, "She brought me to her room for tea."

Corrine slapped the countertop. "She doesn't have a room. I should have known Kathleen would come to see you," Corrine said.

"I don't understand. She doesn't work here?" Mavis asked and bit her lip.

"No. She only comes to those who need her. Hold on a second." Corrine ran behind the counter and brought up a book. "You can read all about her here."

Mavis read the title aloud, "The Ghost of Claire Lake and Hotel Claire," she mumbled. "No."

"Yes." Corrine grinned ear to ear.

"This doesn't make sense. We talked. I touched her hand." Mavis stopped herself. She remembered the cold radiating from Kathleen's skin.

"Did you smell her Jasmine perfume?" Corrine asked.

"I did. It was soft. Comforting." Mavis' headache returned.

"I KNEW IT!" Corrine composed herself. "Count her visit as a blessing. Kathleen knew you only needed a moment."

Drawn to Water

If one were to walk through the little town of Claire Lake, they would see a road with one stoplight, Jacob's Bar and Dinner on the right, the home improvement shop on the left with all the bait and tackle one could need on an outing on the water. Scuttle campground nestled between thick woods and the boat launch. The town burrowed in trees is quickly forgotten when cold weather sends the locals into hibernation. Claire Lake is a town abandoned half the year on the surface, but the locals will never forget the woman who walked into the frozen lake.

I wonder if Kathleen cursed me to this town. Does she have a hold that would kill me if I left? Would I end things without a choice? If one woman choose love over life, what would stop me from making the same decision?

Kathleen breathed in the air of a world untouched by farmlands and billowing smoke from chimneys. The air did not reflect a peat fire burning in the distance. She stared at the ground, nostalgic for home. She knew local indigenous peoples roamed the trees, but the colony leader made a treaty with the chief to keep the peace. Kathleen's family warned that once she left Ireland, returning would be impossible. Within the week, she sat below the deck of a ship with few belongings; her husband spewed the lining of his stomach in a wooden pail next to her feet. She didn't want to leave the rolling hills of green, but Shawn decided the new world meant prosperity. They could raise a family. In small circles, she rubbed her hand over his back.

The new land was not generous. Food was sparse, and the weather turned cold in a blink of an eye. Prosperity was not at hand. Kathleen watched as new mothers screamed and pleaded with God as they brought new children into the new world. Through word, she heard of fathers killing other fathers for food. The want for children dwindled as Kathleen and Shawn struggled to ration out portions for survival. Finally, to surpass the thought of hunger, Shawn stirred the fire while he listened to his wife's soft humming voice from the songs of home. The wind rippled through the uneven cracks of the wooden house and carried fall into winter.

Over a short time, the sparse garden behind the house was robbed twice of vegetables, leaving enough food for a few days. Kathleen knew that she couldn't trust the town's people not to steal. Shawn's strength rapidly disappeared; to stand was an accomplishment. He slept through the fevers that shook his body with cold sweats and vomiting. If Kathleen didn't go into the woods for sustenance, her husband would perish. She would end up with the same fate. When daybreak crept overleaf barren trees, she awoke and pulled herself out from her husband's soft embrace. Shawn's wool jacket swallowed her body as she dressed for the chilly elements. Kathleen loaded a satchel with water and shotgun shells to match the weapon strapped around her shoulders. The door creaked as she slid the door open, but Shawn never moved. Kathleen blew him a kiss and pulled a knitted scarf around her mouth and nose.

All remained quiet as her frozen feet followed the beaten trail to wild berries and possible deer. She had never killed anything before. Kathleen resisted the urge to vomit on her shoes at the thought of warm blood, but she trudged further. Her chapped hands held the jacket closer to her body, but the cold still seeped between her garments and to her goose-bumped skin. The trail seemed longer this trip as she paused every ten minutes or so to listen for creatures nearby.

A clearing ahead propelled Kathleen to move faster. In quick, quiet steps, she stepped over broken tree limbs and dead leaves. Enough rouge remained on the trees to hide her away from the grazing animal insight. The gun in her hands warmed as she loaded the ammunition into the barrel. Her boot caught on a tree root. In a clatter, she dropped the weapon. The creature looked her way as she scrambled to pick the gun up. She shot the deer in the jugular, and the deer fell to the ground. Kathleen ran to the deer and crouched down next to the animal. She stared down at the flea-bitten flesh. From behind, she heard running. *Two feet.* She couldn't believe that a villager would have followed her out to the clearing. She pointed the gun into the woods. A man dressed in animal skins walked to her with hands held out and a sack over his shoulder. He dropped the bag back to her feet. Kathleen didn't break eye contact as she opened the bag to find dry meat inside.

In broken English, he said his name was Saginaw. He said she looked hungry. Kathleen thanked him and pulled the bag over her shoulder with the gun still in hand. She tried to pull the deer by the antlers in her free hand, but the creature did not budge. The man slowly walked to her and dragged the deer. Kathleen's eyes grew wide as her hands went to pull the antlers away. Again, he spoke and told her that he did not want to take it but to help her. Hesitantly, she agreed and led her to her home. She worried that people would see the native man. The agreement said that his people were not to venture into the town.

She was not afraid of this man. Kathleen did not trust him, but she was not scared of him. He pulled the deer to the work shed outside of the house. Still, she held the weapon in her hands as she ran into the house to check on Shawn. He remained in the same place. Shawn's breathing was shallower; his body shook with chills. She tucked more blankets around his weak body. He murmured to his wife, but she couldn't articulate what Shawn was said. Then, slowly, his breathing returned to normal.

Days bled into weeks until Shawn did not recover from his illness. Kathleen remained alone until Saginaw came with meats and edible vegetation. Every day since her husband's death, Saginaw filled the silence ringing through Kathleen's mind. Their relationship was not a verbal one but a series of gestures. Saginaw was never more than a fingertip away; he remained close. Now and again, Saginaw would sing a song from his people's tongue to lull Kathleen asleep. In return, she would tell him fairy tales from Ireland. His visits started like every other day; Saginaw slept in front of the fire on the dirt floor then shared her bed beneath fur blankets. Saginaw pulled her close as she buried her face into the warmth of his embrace.

Kathleen kept him hidden away from the prying eyes of the villagers. After her husband died and her garden disappeared, no one ventured to her little cottage. Her house remained outside the village along the lake, and nobody made way to her doorstep except Saginaw. He lost to his people, cast out of his tribe for helping the white woman. Both were lost to their people and away from their homes. Saginaw comforted her in the new land and made her feel at home. Whenever he left, she longed for his return. A love she never felt for her husband erupted in her soul at every touch and every return with food. At first, she thought her feelings were growing because of the food he would bring, but their friendship meant more than sustenance. Saginaw taught her to hunt, and she taught him to knit.

It had been two days since Saginaw's return, and Kathleen worried something happened to him. It was not like him to disappear for extended periods. She needed to keep her mind busy and away from the thoughts of Saginaw never returning. She needed wool; for the first time in months, Kathleen made her way into the village with dried meat to trade. Kathleen adored the flourishing leaves sprouting from each tree. The grass started to grow back in the fresh, rich green that reminded her of home. Despite not seeing Saginaw, she felt at peace with the world in the spring weather. A chill still seeped through her clothes, but the sun on her face filled her body with warmth.

Kathleen heard a crowd of people whispering and murmuring about something she could not make out. Then, she listened to the booming voice of the village's elected leader speaking loudly. Others inched close to the vote, and Kathleen did the same. She moved behind other people to hear what the commotion was about. The leader spoke out of a trespasser who threatened the lives of the people in the town. He said he'd snuck into a farmer's barn late at night to take milk. The man grew violent when the farmer tried to shoo him away. Neighbors heard the struggle and apprehended the man, and brought him to the town council. The mayor decreed that he was to be hung by the neck until dead on that day for the punishment of this man. Two men dressed in black pulled a hooded man to the hanging post and placed a noose around his neck.

Kathleen saw the bruised brown skin and dark hair under the hood. It was Saginaw. She screamed amongst the crowd and pushed her way to the platform. Tears clouded her vision as she tore through the horde of shouting people. She was almost close to Saginaw when a man dressed in the same drab black held her back. Kathleen struggled against the man and screamed for Saginaw. The mayor looked down at her and cursed her foolishness. Another woman in the crowd explained that Kathleen was still grieving from her dead husband. The man restraining her covered her screaming mouth until she bit down into the soft tissue of his hand. Finally, he let her go, and she ran up to Saginaw's restrained body. She pulled the hood off his head and saw both of his eyes were swollen shut. She kissed him before men dragged her away. For the first time, Saginaw screamed. The crowd grew silent as he called for Kathleen. He cried his love for her. The executioner dropped him to the ground by his neck.

Kathleen ran back to her humble house down the spring path she found beautiful only moments before. She stumbled through the door and flew to the blanket Saginaw used when he slept. His scent still lingered in the fabric when brought to her nose. Her entire world dropped into the abyss. She barely grieved for her husband, but she could not live without the companionship of Saginaw.

Kathleen wrote a letter to whom may visit her cottage. She was forced to come to this land with Shawn, but she made a home with Saginaw. Without him, there was no home, and she would not leave him. Again, she held the blanket to her nose and inhaled his scent before she walked outside. Kathleen dropped the wool jacket she'd been wearing and stepped into the cold water. Her entire body shook with the temperature, but she stared ahead with tears running down her face as she walked further until her body was buried beneath the water. She never came out.

After a time, the townspeople found her drowned body and a letter. In the letter, she told the townspeople her reason for existing was gone. However, she also told the townspeople that they would never leave either as long as her spirit wandered the land. The people of Claire Lake reflect on the story of the woman who was drawn to water. The locals can still hear Saginaw's screams and a woman's cries along the water.

The Hotel Claire stands on that land. The foundation of her home remains in the foundation of the hotel. Kathleen walks along the tree path to the lake, the boat dock constructed many years later, and the halls of Hotel Claire. She can still hear Saginaw's confessions of love through the trees. Kathleen still searches for him.

Mask of Virtue

Villainy wears many masks, but none so dangers as the mask of virtue.

-Sleepy Hollow 1999

Years have passed since Mavis packed the car, left her engagement ring, and ran to a remote town. She wonders about the corridors of the Claire Hotel. Every crack of paint, tear in the carpet, and water-marked nightstand committed to memory. Her need to move away from what she knew is a dog-eared page in the book of her life. She roams the halls parallel to the beings more ancient than the décor. This is the place her child has only known.

Frank, now getting on in age, still lays in the road. Claire lake is where he can't escape the past, the impact of Miriam's daughter, and the friendship with Corrine. The pain of Claire Lake reminds Frank to be thankful for honesty. To be grateful for what he has.

What am I thankful for?

- Nev
- ~~Magnus~~ Too soon. *I may end things.*
- The ability to be that guiding voice for others, but not myself.
- Thumbs and buttons. I think of you often.
- Claire Lake? Why would I be thankful for a place that holds no further value?
- This journal

Why should I stay? Should I end things?

—m—

Theo set down her pen and watched as the sun began to rise over the lake. So she did most sleepless nights—she drank a bottle of wine and fought the chill with Magnus' blanket. His woody musk buried under her nose, another night written away in her journal. Another night she jotted down the stories of this town.

"Have you ever thought about rain? Thought of water memory? The theory is that previous particles from previous substances are found in the water in the lake, in the rain, in the water that we drink. I could be watching waves of urine wash up on the shore. That's not what matters. I haven't discovered what matters," she wrote the last of her thoughts.

Theo stretched. Her back, neck, and shoulders cracked when she reached her arms above her head. An audible ugh escaped between breaths as hips, knees, and toes cracked as she stood. It took a moment for her to move. It always did. When Theo decided to sit amongst sparse light, her legs tucked under her, her body always paid the price. Pain.

Another empty wine bottle. Theo hated throwing out the BlackBerry Merlot bottles. She swore one day she would use them to make vases or mosaics—the reflection of light through wine-stained glass. Thick grime layered her teeth; the pack of cigarettes remained on her breath. Theo passed the clock as she walked through the sliding glass doors. Seven AM.

I have an hour before my first appointment.

A light knock; Theo walked over and opened the door. Mrs. Coleman was on time as usual.

"Good morning, Theo." Greying curls blew around Mrs. Coleman's face as she stepped inside the door. Then, finally, she spoke, "You didn't sleep last night, did you?"

"I think it's my job to do the analysis?" Theo said; she wrapped her ripped plaid robe around her waist.

"I'm just your secretary, but it doesn't hurt for the doctor to talk about her feelings as well," Mrs. Coleman said and draped her coat over the arm of the coach.

"You know that you're more than a secretary, Nell. I recall thirty years of friendship before we opened this private practice."

"Well, I guess, keep your friends close and your enemies closer... yada, yada, yada," Nell laughed and dug into her bag for the appointment book. She found the day's schedule and spoke, "I hope you're not planning to bury me in the backyard. Ripped robe and messy hair, you look like Mort Reiny. You should probably brush your teeth before your first appointment at eight."

"Who?" Theo asked and pulled her robe closer.

"Stephen King? The movie?" Nell shook her head as Theo remained oblivious. "Uncultured," Nell laughed as she spoke.

"I've recently decided to let my teeth rot and fall out," Theo said; she placed her hands on her hips and stared straight onto Nell.

"I don't think a patient would feel confident in a psychiatrist with rotting teeth and bad breath," Nell said and headed to her desk. "You should probably brush your hair and change out of your robe while you're at it."

"You're probably right," Theo said.

"I know I am." Nell's voice carried to Theo's bedroom, "Tic Toc!"

—⟨⟩—

Theo found that her patients liked her voice. They liked the way she spoke, but not too much. She didn't wear clothes with flare or heavy jewelry; Theo barely allowed herself to wear her wedding ring. The minor use it did. The room she held these conversations in was decorated but not personal. The space kept as close to unbiased as possible. It wasn't her job to distract her patients with décor but to perform cognitive therapy. She wanted to know more about these people and why they stay in Claire Lake. Theo wanted to know why she stayed.

—⟨⟩—

"I dreamt about him last night," Danny said, then continued, "It was different."

"How so? Tell me what happened?" Theo leaned further into her seat and rested her forearm on the side of the chair.

Danny leaned forward and held his head in his hands. "He talked. The Creeper talked."

"What did the creature say?" she asked.

123

"He said I should end things," Danny uttered and looked towards Theo.

I may end things. "What do you think he meant?" Theo asked.

"I don't know. After he spoke, the Creeper grabbed the sides of my head and stared deep into my eyes," he said.

"Could you feel his hands?" Theo asked.

Danny's voice sounded distant, "Yes. They crushed my head. I couldn't move."

"What else did you see?" she asked.

"I saw my eyes," Danny said. He opened his eyes and stared down at his hands. "I saw my lips and nose. He wore a mask of my skin. This was all before he licked my face. His eyes rolled back."

"What happened next?" Theo asked.

"I woke up. I pulled myself out of that dream." He rubbed his eyes.

"Danny, do you dream of the creeper when you're stressed?" Theo knew the answer, but she wanted him to respond.

"You know I do, Dr. Theo." He stood from his chair and moved to her bookshelf. Danny asked, "Do you read these?"

She snapped her fingers. "Focus, Danny. What has been causing stress lately?"

"I decided to finish college," he said and sat back down.

"That's fantastic! You've talked about going back for so long." Theo wrote *college* down in the journal. "What is causing you stress?" she asked.

"I decided to go to Pittsburgh for school."

"That is a significant distance. Thiel was only twenty minutes away, and you thought that was a great distance. So what made you decide, Pittsburgh?" Theo held her pen to her chin.

"I want to get out of here. I am so tired of living in a place with no life. It's gorgeous now; people are headed to Pumpkin Fest, but then the decay of winter sets in. I'm ready for something more exciting than Kady's Ice Cream opening in the spring," he exasperated.

Theo spoke, "The decision's been made. You know what you want and what you don't want. So what is stressing you?"

"I guess Poppy. We talked about moving to Pittsburgh. Before, she was excited to apartment hunt, to decorate, to live somewhere new. Now that this is becoming a reality, she's not sure if she wants to leave. She says her life is here. I ask her what life is, and she never has a straight answer," he said in frustration.

"Have you considered that Poppy is comfortable here?" Theo asked. "Her family is here."

"Doc. I want to start a life with her. I've carried a ring in my pocket for months." Danny pulled the black velvet box from his pocket. He held it up and asked, "What if she doesn't want to share that life with me?"

"I think it will do you both good to talk about Pittsburgh. Tell her how you feel. I would never sway you away from finishing school and leaving Claire Lake, but I think it's important for you to decide what is important to you," Theo said and wrapped the leather cord around her journal.

A knot formed in her back while she talked with her patient. The interlocking air pocket in her vertebrae cracked as Theo stretched out her body. His story, his memory of that night drew her in. Danny suffered night terrors and insomnia. Theo looked over her shorthand of his visits.

- Young child holding hands with mother
- The cousin Amber
- Christmas
- Substance abuse of the cousin
- Gerbil slaughtered
- Danny's first encounter with death
- "Superstitions" created
- The Creeper
- Masked behind his facial features
- School
- Poppy
- Fear of self and decisions

Her pen retraced "Creeper" on her notes. She wondered what it meant to believe in something out there, something watching or predicting a person's decisions. Theo redirected her thoughts, not God; she still questioned his motives for her life. Danny built his life around the superstitions created of that Christmas. A time of year meant to rejoice in the company of family and friends.

Nell knocked and opened the door, "Theo, you have an appointment with Charlie McCoy today."

"Thank you. What time is her appointment?" Theo asked. She stood and walked over to Charlie's journal on the shelf.

"Four o'clock. Before you dig into Charlie's case, lunch, we should go to Lago Winery. We could get a white pizza and a glass of Pino Grigio," Nell suggested.

"I thought we should go to Hotel Claire for Pumpkin Soup and homemade bread from Kathleen's," Theo remarked.

"Smart idea! We can get there before Pumpkin Fest takes over the hotel," Nell said. "Oh, while you were with Danny, Magnus called."

"Did he leave a message?" Theo asked.

"On the answering machine. I didn't listen to it," Nell replied.

"I'll listen to it later. Are you ready to go?" Theo asked and stepped out of her office. She gathered her coat and wallet.

"Whenever you are boss." Nell followed suit with Theo.

Theo thought her mother was her most significant burden, but then there was Magnus. He was supposed to be her anchor, locked in a marriage that no longer sustained water. Theo guessed her vows to her husband were her most immense burden. Magnus stepped away from those promises. He had no problem moving when Nev went to college. She thought of this on the drive to Hotel Claire. The first time in twenty-two years, she drove to Kathleen's, and the first time she went without Magnus.

After all these years, she still remembered her vows. They were burned into her memory. So the vows stung when Magnus packed luggage to live the next town over. He said it was easier to move there for work. "Twenty minutes," Theo said aloud.

"What did you say?" Nell asked.

"Oh...I was thinking how long it usually takes to get the food." Theo made a poor attempt at patting her belly. "I'm starving," she said over a growling stomach.

Her wedding vows ran through her thoughts.

I promise to love you with a love,
That is more than love.
But, why do I love you?
Let me tell you the ways.

You're explosive personality and contagious laughter.
Your inexhaustible hands lift and carry a day's work but still carry warmth.
Your passion for a visual story—who would have thought this would all start with a film set, a zombie, and some makeup?
The soothing sound of your heart when you hold me close.
I will never grow exhausted by your words of adoration.

I promise to love, accept, and cherish the moments we share.
We all go a little mad sometimes,
But I know you'll be there to pick me up.

Theo repeated those meaningless words. The line of traffic to the festival, to the hotel, stretched a mile. Theo wondered if they should have gone to Lago instead.

"You're very quiet," Nell said and repositioned her purse on her lap.

"I've been thinking of Charlie. But, you know, she's visited me a couple of times, and I have yet to hear her speak." Theo tapped her thumbs on the steering wheel.

"Is it inappropriate to ask what Vera says is wrong with her?" Nell asked.

"I guess I can make an exception due to hearsay from my client's mother." Theo gathered information about Charlie from her bank of memory and continued, "Vera said that Charlie was eight when she started acting out. Her behavior included listening and responding to imaginary friends."

"That sounds harmless. I remember having an imaginary friend when I was little," Nell said.

"Did your imaginary friend appear as your dead father?" Theo glanced over.

Nell tilted her head and made brief eye contact. "No. I can't say they did."

Theo spoke, "So I've been told by Vera, Charlie reacted violently to her attempts to make this friend disappear. I believe what Charlie has seen all these years has transformed into a sort of agoraphobia."

"Can you elaborate on this?" Nell asked.

Theo felt reluctant to share more, but none of this came from the mouth of Charlie. "If she is away from the house too long. Reportedly, anxiety attacks follow shortly after. She has attempted self-harm."

"Jeez. Poor kid," Nell sighed and starred out the passenger window.

"Poor kid," Theo sighed as well. She inched the car to the hotel.

—〰—

Vibrant leaves crunched under Theo's booties. She could smell candied nuts and cider from vendors parked along the path to the Hotel. Her stomach growled, and her mouth watered. Theo could feel the crunch of brown sugar candied cashews, washed down with hot cider and cinnamon stick. The urge to buy maple cotton candy almost consumed her. *Maybe later.*

"Don't forget the pumpkin drop. Don't forget the one-ton pumpkin drop over a school bus. Get your tickets to be in the splash zone," A man announced over a megaphone.

"I don't know about you, but I love being covered in pumpkin guts!" Nell looped her arm through Theo's and giggled as they walked over the gravel path.

"Oh, I'm sure," Theo said through a half-hearted laugh.

Hundreds of people jammed in one space allowed Theo to understand why people could feel claustrophobic at festivals—the invasion of personal space, unwanted conversation, and the literal stepping on toes could give anyone pause. All of these people would disappear when the leaves disappeared. Soon the tourist and visitors to Claire Lake would forget they exist. Theo almost felt sorry that the town would soon be forgotten in a colorless landscape. No life. *I may end things.*

—⚹—

Hotel Claire still took Theo's breath away. On the lawn, she could still see the aisle made of rouge and orange leaves. Theo still felt the weight of orange roses, and plum sprigs of blossoms tucked away in the cream satin bouquet holder—the alter draped with tulle, lace, and white roses, and how could she forget the way Magnus stared at her as she walked down the aisle. It may have been the veil clouding her vision, but she swore he held back tears. *He hasn't looked at me like that in years.* That was before Miriam cheated on Frank and before Charlie was a thought. *Twenty-two-years-ago.*

"Oh my God. I'm so hungry! Good thing you didn't book your next appointment until four," Nell interrupted.

"We would have never made it through the crowd quickly," Theo said and led the way through the Hotel's main entrance. People with luggage, a crying baby, juxtaposed the vintage décor. Printed signs set on easels advertised ghost tours and printed copies of The Ghost of Claire Lake and Hotel Claire.

"What fun! We should sign up," Nell suggested and nudged Theo.

"I thought you were hungry?" Theo questioned.

"I am, but we could do that after lunch. We still have plenty of time to kill," Nell said.

"I don't know. I've been on that tour enough that I could give it to you for free." Theo began to pull away.

"Come on. It'll be fun." Nell pulled Theo back. She said, "I'll pay. It's ten bucks for both of us. Besides, I've never been on it."

"If you insist." Theo tried to reject the smile creeping on her face. Instead, she led Nell to the sign-up sheet.

—⚹—

Waiters in black uniforms and black shoes squeaked across the freshly waxed wooden floors. The bulk of the crowd remained among the festivities outside. Kathleen's remained steady with ongoing customers, but lines for refined food were not out the doors. Fine linen white tablecloths, fall foliage, and wildflower arrangements decorated each table.

Theo unfolded her silverware from her napkin and placed it on her lap. She was ready for another glass of water and a glass of Sauvignon Blanc when the waiter came for food orders.

"I know that we're eating lunch, but I could still go for some garbage fries after the tour." Nell gulped water.

Theo crossed and uncrossed her ankles. She felt strange being here, but she stirred up a conversation, "Hmm…candied cashews. I'm going to get some for later."

"Maybe they're your secret ingredient to sleep." Nell crossed her arms from across the table.

"I think that's Melatonin," Theo said through laughter. She took the last sip of her complimentary water.

"When was the last time you slept soundly?" Nell asked.

"Mmmm…19 years ago, before Nev was born," Theo said; she and glanced around to find their waiter.

"You've slept since the birth of your daughter! I'm serious. Have you slept since Magnus moved to his apartment?" Nell asked.

I may end things—a deep sigh released through Theo's parted lips. "Not really," Theo admitted. Her eyes met Nell's, and she said, "My house is too quiet. I only have my thoughts to keep me company. It's easier to nap during the day than to lay awake in my bed wishing I could sleep, wondering if Nev is safe, or wondering where lost things could be hiding in my house." Theo held the base of her glass and tapped her finger on the edge. She continued, "Recently, I've been writing at night. I've been writing about the people of this town."

"That's a lot to take in. First off, Nev is fine. I don't think she could survive without talking to you. Secondly, you are driving yourself nuts about unnecessary things. Put yourself in that happy place. Isn't that the advice you give your clients?" Nell asked.

"I do. It's easier to be that guiding voice for others, but I tend to allow myself to fall through the cracks. However, you're right," Theo said.

"I know I am because I know you. We're close." Nell reached and held Theo's hand. She spoke, "You're allowed to be troubled. Just because you're the doctor doesn't mean you don't need to talk about things." Nell cleared her throat and changed the subject. "So, what have you been writing about?" she asked.

Theo almost felt embarrassed to tell her what she spends her nights writing about. "Well, I've spent a lot of time in this town with my family. Nev grew up here. You've lived here long enough to know everything about everyone. So…" Theo took a breath and said, "I decided to write about the people. There is more to unearth about this town than the surface-level summertime tourist trap. So I wrote about the pain this town has suffered."

Nell's brows rose. "You wrote about your clients?" she asked.

"No. I could only wish I could get these people in my chair." Theo bit her bottom lip.

"So hold on. I'm confused. What did you write about?" Nell asked and tilted her head.

"I wrote about the town's gossip. I gave life to those stories, and I tried to create a reason for those actions. I've been trying to understand why people stay in this town."

Nell leaned in, "Is there gossip about me? Do I have a story?"

A genuine laugh erupted from Theo. "No! I'm sorry, Nelly. I have no dirt to dish about you."

"That's a shame." Nell whispered, "You don't know everything about me. My name's not Nell." Both women laughed. A new waiter came around to deliver the food ordered a half-hour before.

"Mrs. Shirley! Where's Mr. Shirley?" the waiter directed his question to Theo.

"Nice to see you, Max." Heat and color rose in her face. Then, she spoke, "He, unfortunately, went out of town for business."

"That's a shame! You've never missed a date at Kathleen's," he said, then filled their water glasses. "Well, happy anniversary!" Max gathered his tray walked back towards the kitchen.

"How could I be so stupid?" Nell's face was priceless. Her mouth agape, and brows rose. "How could I have forgotten your anniversary?"

"Ne.." Theo tried to finish, but Nell stopped her from finishing.

"Why the hell are we here? Hold on." Nell put her hand up and redirected her question, "Why did you come here today?"

"I thought this is what I wanted," Theo paused. "I didn't know how I would feel."

"Did you hurt yourself?" Nell asked.

"Not more than usual. Nell, my entire life flipped; nothing has been the same. But today...today I wanted to feel some semblance of normalcy. It was wrong to follow this particular tradition. I thought it would make me feel better to face this without him, but I was wrong. Being here sets my skin on fire. Every inch of this place brings back memories. So yes, Nell, I did hurt myself." Theo recrossed her ankles and starred out the window that overlooked the lake.

"Theo, I love you. I've been with you for everything, but this is something you need to work out. You have heard what I thought of Magnus. You heard what I thought when he moved out. You heard what I thought when he denied a separation and divorce. I want you to think about what you want." Nell stood from the table and kissed Theo on the forehead. She said, "Remember that I love you. I am canceling your four o'clock appointment."

Theo began to stand, but Nell nudged her back down.

"Where are you going?" Theo asked.

"I am grabbing my garbage fries, and then I'm going home. I will see you in the morning," Nell said and walked away.

Theo turned in her chair. "How are you getting home?" she asked. "I drove."

"I'll figure it out, but I want you to take a moment for yourself," Nell said and walked out of the restaurant.

Late afternoon sun showed through the mosaic of leaves decorating maple trees along with the hotel. Theo sat, she thought; she tapped her wine glass. She didn't know what she wanted. Her soup had grown cold, but Theo couldn't stomach the thought of eating anything. The engrossing aroma of cider and fair food turned sour. She wasn't in the mood.

Theo didn't wait for the bill; she left enough cash to cover her bill and tip. The hotel left an unfamiliar feeling. In a brief instant, Theo wasn't sure where to go. Magnus always led the way. Her feet led the way back to the crowded lobby. Excited tourists waited for the tour guide to arrive. Theo forgot about the tour. She looked towards the main entrance but decided to stay. The tour was already paid for.

Ahead of the group stood Frank. Clean-shaven and showered, Frank stood at the front of the group with a mag light held in the air. Theo walked to the front of the group to greet him.

"Hi. I didn't realize you would be giving the tour," Theo smiled.

"I had promised me fifty-bucks a trip plus tips," he laughed. "Where's the mister? I haven't seen him around lately."

"He's been swamped. I haven't seen him a lot either." She could feel the heat in her face again.

"For you, Theo, I promise a good tour." Frank flashed the light and shouted to the crowd of eager people, "Let's get this thing started. If you're not signed up for the tour, kindly stay behind. You can buy your tickets at the desk for the next one." Frank led the group past the ballroom. Theo tried to advert her eyes away from that room. She still saw herself bathed in the moonlight as Magnus waltzed around the floor. No music. Just the sound of his humming and her laughter. Breathing became difficult; she didn't want to cry.

"This way, everyone! Scooch close. This hall is a little narrow," Frank said.

A little girl stood close to Theo. Smiled down at her, but she could tell the child was nervous. She reminded Theo of Nev when she was that small. *A brave little girl.* The group came to a halt.

The child looked up at Theo and motioned her to bend down. "Will the ghosts hurt us?" she whispered.

"No. They're just as curious about us as we are of them," Theo whispered back.

Frank brought the group to a set of outdated stairs. "Guest isn't usually allowed on these, but it's ok for the tour." He brought out a bunch of index cards and read, "Guest have reported sightings of a little boy running up and down these stairs. They will feel a tug on their hands or their clothes. Some have reported the boy asking where his mother is. This is the spot where a boy named Xavier fell down the stairs and broke his neck. Our records show Xavier was the son of a maid who worked here. The date of his death is a little fuzzy." For a moment, Theo wondered if the child she just spoke to was real. Then, when she looked down, she saw the girl holding a woman's hand.

The group went up to the second floor. Different rooms had small gold plates nailed to the doors—inscriptions of the gold plates detailed names of people who donated money to restore the hotel. Frank stopped at a room at the end of the hall. Flowers came to Theo's thought; she swore she could smell Jasmine.

"This is our next stop and probably our most famous spot." Frank switched index cards and continued, "This is the room of the lonely bride. Many stories speculate that her name was Kathleen. There are stories that she was a bride who died the night of her wedding. Our history is a little unclear of this part of the hotel. Many years ago, Hotel Claire suffered a major fire that burnt down part of it. Many of the records were destroyed. However, this area is the oldest part of Hotel Claire. So, who died in this area? We're not sure," Frank stated. He took a moment to pause and catch his breath. "Guest have reported being visited late at night by a woman. All of those guests have been women. One guest reported that a woman appeared in her room and sat on the bed. The guest's mother recently past and she was distraught. The ghostly women soothed her and then disappeared. It's also been reported that a flowery scent follows her."

Theo followed the group to the rest of the hotel. Frank told the group about the soldier who was shot during a battle, the elder couple who dances in their room, and the man who rummages through the guests' luggage. Theo was pleasantly surprised to hear about new encounters. In all the years she stayed, she'd never experienced anything supernatural. Perhaps she was too skeptical. If anything, the tour distracted Theo. She still couldn't believe Frank would give the tour. Theo dug in her wallet for a twenty to provide him with.

"That is the end of the tour. I hope you all enjoyed the haunted history of Hotel Claire. If you want a more ghostly history of this place, you can buy the book downstairs at the desk. Ask for Corrine," Frank shouted.

Frank held a jar out to people as they exited the tour. Theo was the last to drop her tip in.

"Very generous, Theo." Frank pulled out the twenty and held it up, and said, "Much appreciated!"

"Super interesting! I'll have to retake your tour next year," Theo said.

"That's if Corrine doesn't fire me," Frank chimed. "Tell your hubby we should get drinks sometime."

"I'll pass the message along." *I may end things.* She wanted to shout those words to anyone who mentioned Magnus. But, she didn't dare to tell anyone other than Nell.

—⟋⟍—

Theo made the reservation earlier in the week to stay in the honeymoon suite. *Their suite.* Two months passed, and still, no sit-down, no conversation of future, no consoling words. She was in the dark and too afraid to confront uncertainty.

She walked the halls passing happy voices of children, a man talking loudly into a phone, a group of voices making plans for festival activities, and the wafting scent of Jasmine. Theo stared at the floor and watched as her feet took each careful step. She wanted to walk and think but not think *I may end things.*

She walked to the ballroom. A light glow came from the corner. Broken glass, the shattering of a dish broke to her left, but she saw herself, young and dancing in the dark. She was stripped down to her white lace bra and panties as Magnus twirled her around. They danced to the music of his serenade. His lips touched her neck as his fingers traced the outline of her panties. She fell into his arms laughing. They hadn't made it back to their suite for round two. There they lay, intertwined and unbreakable next to a cracked champagne bottle and two glass flutes.

"Can I help you?" The voice interrupted the memory.

Theo looked again to see an empty ballroom and the glow from the bar. "Sorry. I know, the ballroom is closed," Theo said.

"No. You're good, Mrs. Shirley! I'm just cleaning up." Mavis swept around the bar. "Do you want a drink? It's on the house," Mavis called.

"How about a left-over bottle of Bourbon, a small glass, and a little ice?" Theo asked. She sat on the barstool. Between countless bottles of liquor, she could see herself. The warm glow from the bar did not hide the bags under Theo's eyes; she wasn't sure she'd ever sleep again. She scrubbed her hands against the soft tissue of her cheeks.

"A busy night tonight?" Theo smirked as Mavis poured the Bourbon into the highball glass.

"The Psychic Fair cleaned out pretty quickly. People got their readings, drank their fill, and then stumbled out." Mavis took a wet rag and wiped up previous booze stains from the event.

"How much do I owe you for the bottle?" Theo asked. She dug into her wallet. "I have two twenty's and a ten that have been in here for a long time."

"Your credit is always good here, Doc," Mavis said and put away clean glasses.

"Please, call me, Theo." She took a drink and continued, "I may be ending the whole *Mrs. Shirley thing.*"

Mavis stopped, "Oh no. I'm so sorry."

"It's ok. No one knows. I'm not even sure if I know." Theo swished the Bourbon around her glass.

"Was it someone else?" Mavis asked.

"No. Nothing like that. I think we just got tired of each other. We got too comfortable," Theo paused. "He said it would be easier for work if he moved out for a bit. So I supported him because I love him so much." She took another drink and continued, "After we moved into our new house, moved my mom in, later after her passing I started my practice from home, then everything changed. Magnus was busy all the time. He wasn't there to help me."

Mavis leaned her body against the bar top. "Well, I'll be damned. I never thought you two of all people would cut ties."

"They're not completely severed. Hanging on by a thread, but not cut," Theo said.

Mavis remained quiet for a moment while Theo poured another glass. "You know, I heard about you two when I first moved to Claire Lake. I was told about the couple who got caught in here on the night of their wedding. You two still come back every year."

Theo smirked and said, "Came back. That was a long time ago," she giggled. "What a night. You're right, though; we were caught, wrapped in nothing but a tablecloth. Magnus knew the security guard. With a smirk, the guard sent us back to our suite. Whenever we see him at the hotel, we share a smile and a simple greeting." Theo tapped her glass, ready for another. *But, again, that was a long time ago.*

"I hope to be remembered like that," Mavis said.

"How long have you been in Claire Lake?" Theo asked. Her phone vibrated in her pocket. *Magnus.* Theo sent the call to voicemail.

"Hmm...Three years this spring," Mavis said.

Theo wasn't sure if it was the booze or her need to know the answer, but she asked, "Mavis, why do you stay in Claire Lake?"

Mavis grabbed a glass from the shelf and poured herself some leftover red wine. "I grew up in a town like this, country. Then I decided I wanted to become a city person. That didn't last long. I realized I didn't want to go home, but I also didn't want to live in a place taller than trees. Claire Lake is home for me. I'm comfortable here."

"Really?" Theo asked.

"Yeah." Mavis' voice softened, "In the city, people wouldn't look in your direction twice. I was just a female stock character trying to live a boho life in a city full of people doing the same thing. There was nothing original or unique about me or my interests," she said; she leaned against the bar.

"You." Theo pointed to Mavis and asked, "Not original? As soon as you came to town, you gave people whiplash."

"You see me," Mavis smiled.

"I just observe and say what I see," Theo said; she tapped her glass for a refill.

Mavis emptied the bottle. "You don't just observe," Mavis placed her hand over Theo's, "You make the people of this town feel seen. I stay because Claire Lake lets me be who I want to be."

137

"Lately, I just feel cold," Theo placed her hands on her arms, "as I'll never get warm," Theo said. *I may end things.*

"Are you coming down with something, Doc?" Mavis asked as she placed her hand over Theo's forehead.

Theo pushed her hand away. "It's nothing like that. Lately, all around me is cold. I can find no warmth. There is not one thing I am looking forward to; I watch the sun rise and fall. Right now, I can't even tell you what I enjoy.

"Being here," Theo pointed her fingers to the bar, "only brings back memories of when I was pleased. I can't tell you the last time I've felt that."

"Don't mind me asking this, Theo, but when did this start?" Mavis asked.

"Probably when I moved mom in. I knew I was overwhelmed and depressed, but I didn't think much of it because I was too busy running around doing stuff for her," Theo said.

"God rest, Saoirse," Mavis said as she bowed her head.

"I miss her every day," Theo said as she too bowed her head. "I felt stronger with her here. Even to the end, she didn't remember who I was, but I still felt better then."

"She will be missed," Mavis said.

"You know, when Magnus left," Theo held Mavis' eyes, "I was ok with it. I figured if he didn't want to stay, there was no use in forcing him. When he left, though, he took every bit of warmth from my body. I can't sleep at night because I wake up freezing, then I start thinking, and then the sun rises. Time to do it all over again."

"Do you miss him?" Mavis asked.

I may end things. "Yes. Very much." Theo massaged her temples.

"You should tell him," Mavis said as she continued to clean the bar.

I may end things. "I can't," Theo said.

Mavis slung the dry rag over her shoulder. "Why not?"

He may end things. "I don't know if I'm ready to hear him say it's over." Theo dug into her wallet for her twenties and placed them on the bar.

"Do what will give you peace," Mavis said as she picked up the cash. "I said it was on the house."

"It's for the therapy session," Theo said as she picked up a handful of napkins and a pen.

The night stretched across the lake hours before. Across the water and sporadic trees, Theo could see the last of the year's campfires; by the next week, all would be gone. She held a few borrowed napkins and a pen from the bar. Creaking floorboards broke the silence of subtle waves as Theo followed the boardwalk to the water. Candied nuts and cider still lingered in the wind. *Tomorrow, those treats are mine.*

Theo sat on the edge of the dock. The air grew cold without the sun, but Theo didn't mind. Every star reflected their age and traveled across the glass of the lake. The wood creaked under her butt when she pulled her phone from her back pocket; her notifications showed two calls from Magnus and a voicemail. Air entered and exhaled slowly through Theo's nose. *Not yet.*

Brightness from Theo's phone pierced the dark. In one hand, she held her phone for light, and the other had a pen over a napkin. Theo wrote, "I was innocent before I touched the lake, brought that water to my lips. I could never return now—now that I've tasted the Earth of this tainted town. The opportunity was there. I could have left when Magnus refused to stay in Claire Lake. I didn't expect to stay in *his* hometown. Now, I've tasted the fruit. I am stuck."

Those words burned her fingers. They were false. Theo balled up the napkin and threw it into the water. Her breath lay heavy on her chest. *Why am I here?* Theo tried again,

"Magnus,

I've changed since being here. Things I thought I knew changed. Perspective is everything. When I thought I tasted the land, I was wrong. Claire Lake took a bite of me, chewed me up, and spat out humanity. I understand what it means to lose everything, my mom, my comfortable life, and myself. The people of this town stay not because they are too stuck to move or too ignorant to leave. They remain because

Claire Lake reminds them what it means to be human. They stay as a reminder to be themselves.

I stayed to be close to your embrace, your selfishness, and your laughter. There was a time where I didn't need coffee or wine; I just needed you. A long time ago, you were the person who understood me the most. You were the person I let into my razor wire, but then you became the person who knew me the least. I stayed in this town with you because I hoped that you would remember the stranger in your bed—the stranger who fills your coffee cup every morning. I can't make you stay in Claire Lake, but that doesn't mean I have to leave. We built a life here, and I intend on living my life. Whether that's with you and our daughter or with just Nev." Theo flipped the napkin over. "I'm here for me."

Theo folded the napkin and stuck it back in her pocket. She continued to stare out across the lake. "I'm not ready to end things," Theo said aloud. Candied fall treats wafted across the lawn of Hotel Claire. As soon as the smell was there, it was replaced by the delicensing of Jasmine. Theo closed her eyes and breathed deeply. A spiderweb of tingles stretched across her shoulders; Theo leaned in. *I'm here for me.* A tinge of warmth lingered over her skin, subtle but present.

"In the end, we're all ghosts in Claire Lake. We can never leave, nor do we want to," Theo wrote in her journal. She wrapped the leather cord to bind the pages. Then, her fingers reached for the nightside lamp. Theo pulled the cord and left only moonlight through her bedroom window. Her goal was to sleep at least five hours in her bed.

"Baby steps," Theo whispered to the dark.

I may not end things.

Epilogue: Thanksgiving

Many years later, Frank gripped the handles of the rocking chair. Amish wood struck the concrete garage floor. He said nothing but instead observed the sky shift; clouds revealed sparse stars and the coexistence of sun and moon in one sky. In glances, I saw the view behind me. However, the shift of time in the atmosphere became unfamiliar. I watched the shadows consume jumper cables, hard hats, extension cords, rakes, and brooms hanging on rusted hooks. Shelves of tools disappeared in the growing darkness. Among us sat a mustard yellow Porsche dusted with age. Frank, Steve, and Poppy sat in the portrait of my view. Shadows produced inky pigments beneath their chairs.

My eyes turned to focus on the three seated before me. Steve threw his head back in hilarity, slapped his knee, and took another drag of the cigarette. My body was glued to the chair and incapable of such quick gestures. Gravity fixated on my legs, shoulders, and fingers. It was a mistake to sit atop the curve of the driveway. I feared tumbling, breaking through the lawn chair, cracking my flesh on the cement. I was Humpty Dumpty, never to be put together again.

Poppy asked, "Can you feel it?"

I confessed, "I'm lost in thought."

My words felt unusual when I spoke. Was I making sense? Was I making too much sense? Was I making a spectacle of myself? Instead of fidgeting hands, I watched Steve›s lips when he chuckled with his mother. She mimicked the same sincerity. This was a visit way overdue; mother and son chatted, smoked, and joked. Anything heavy on the mind was thrown out the window; only fresh air and welcome contentment was allowed in this space.

Frank and I shared silence. He sat in his rocker without a word to expose. I fixated mother and son's smirk. What a wonderful thing to see one another's mouths move when they talk. I realized how much I needed to see people's faces. I didn't just see them, but I saw their words—their story.

Poppy watched me as she chuckled. Her sparkle buried beneath skin tanned by the pool, her life raising two sons, and losing a daughter close to birth. I saw her.

She turns to Steve. "Morgan is stoned out of her gourd."

I laugh. It's true; the fumes of a vape pen narrowed my perspective.

Steve says, "I would rather have a drink."

The conversation lasted hours, days, or even years. It's only been ten minutes, so, I'm told. Gramps continued rocking to the beat of his thoughts. He stared not at the neighbor across the street, but at the memory of his wife, at the memory of a time he could drive himself. All the while, Steve and Poppy shared stories.

"I would rather have a drink," Steve said.

"Not me. I'd rather smoke," Poppy said. "Especially the giggly stuff."

More laughter and fireworks explode in the plethora of memory spilled between the two. I couldn't keep up.

"I told Gia to keep an eye on me in case I started to look too suspicious," Steve said. Creases by his eyes deepened when he spoke.

My mouth tingled.

"Danny and I sat on the beach. A patrol quad went by, and I yelled, 'He has weed! He has weed!' I thought he was going to die. Glad we were sitting by the water because I wet my chair." Poppy sipped from her mug.

Their stories felt like memories. Every detail down to what Steve wore; He dressed in his black uniform, matching apron, non-slip black shoes. A splash of fry grease and chopped onion replaced a woody musk. The only speck of color exposed was the red trim around his sleeves and the teal calm waters whirlpooling into his pupils. I pictured Poppy sun-absorbed, red frozen margarita, and a stream of pee in her aqua beach chair.

"There was a night I made Granny's chicken soup recipe. The next morning an empty soup tub and spoon sat on the counter." Poppy lit a cigarette.

"That was the night I went to my bedroom straight from work. It was like ten, and you came in to say goodnight. Well," Steve paused to catch his breath. "Before you came in, I'd just eaten part of an edible. Then I heard you coming up the stairs. So, I freaked out and pushed all of the crumbs under the blanket."

"Oh, God." She giggled.

"I had the munchies so bad. I ran down the stairs trying not to make any noise," he was laughing so hard, "but the stairs sounded like bombs going off every time I moved."

"You ate the chicken soup!"

Steve snorted and almost dropped from his chair.

"Yes, I was too afraid to tell you. So, I blamed the cat," Steve said.

These memories felt familiar but fresh all at once. Steve had a way of capturing the moment; more importantly, I remembered what gravitated me to him, humor. Marriage dulled our spontaneity, but his spirit reminded me of how we met. He held me in conversation and captivated my mind. It couldn't be possible a person with personality, a talent for character voices, and creativity could be turned down by another. I loved him, and at that moment, I remembered why we said, 'I do.'

Mrs. Doubtfire, Annie Wilks, *Golden Girls*, and Nancy from *The Craft* all projected from his lips. Every one of these characters brought me to applause as he reenacted beloved scenes. He could have gone places with all this talent, made millions, but instead, he chose a life with me. Instead of celebrity events, we talk about names for future children, the house we hope to afford, and holidays with family. He chose me instead of a career that could support him in ways I cannot. That night, I remembered why we vowed our lives to one another. Still, guilt holds a grip on my brain. I wonder if he would leave me, or worse, regret the life we built.

Time occurred to me. *How long have we been sitting here? How long have I been staring dry-eyed at Steve as he reenacted the dance from Titanic?* Bubbled up from my gut, a blurt of laughter exploded. I laughed.

Uncontrolled, untethered by the weight of social politeness. I couldn't stop. Then, I remembered the lawn chair. Stop. Stop. Stop laughing. I'm going to fall. Stop laughing. Stop being rude.

"Grandma is dead." No. Too soon. I can't cry in front of them again.

"What did you say?" Steve asked.

Teal ocean waters drowned me. I felt the waves of his irises tickle my toes, wash salty tides over my reached-out fingers. I was on that beach with him, taking in every ray of light across the sky; the tannest I'd ever been. Finally, my dad, my culture, would be proud I look like them. They wouldn't abandon me. Years of bleach, hours inside, green eyes, I was a piece that didn't fit. There was one, someone I coincided with, Grandma.

"She's dead," I said aloud.

Steve stood in front of me and leaned down. "Morgan, I can't understand what you're saying."

I touched the dead skin layering my mouth. "Can I have some water? In a plastic cup? I'm afraid I'll drop a glass." Then, mechanically, I peeled away the skin away from my lips. I tried to smile, but cotton filled my mouth and turned my teeth to sandpaper.

Steve reached out and patted the leg I didn't know was bouncing.

Poppy stood from her chair and grabbed his walker. "I need to take Gramps in for his bath. I can't believe he hasn't gone in. yet." Frank came to his feet without much complaint.

Steve also stood and kissed my head. "I'll be right back with your water."

A moment ago, the chairs held life. The fabric was warmed by their bodies, by the blood flowing through a network of veins. Then nothing. The rocker and two lawn chairs sat empty, facing the sky. I was left alone for hours, for days. I thought about being alone, what my family felt when I left, how my mom felt when dad left. Was I becoming him? I know being here impacted, my family. I know being here affected, Grandma. She died when I wasn't there; fortunately, I got to say goodbye the weekend before. Still, saying goodbye wasn't enough. I wasn't there to soothe her when she begged for help; I wasn't there when her screams filled the house during bath times; I wasn't there when she remembered us. Yes, I said goodbye, but I wasn't there to feel her hand pat mine one last time.

In an instant, I blinked. There Steve was; he held a faux plastic glass out to me. With both hands, I received the offering. A simple notion that spoke to me, the cup of water, meant, "I care."

"Thank you," I managed to say between gulps of water.

Steve beamed in the same way, he did before sex; Steve grinned at the suggestion of Chinese take-out or the *F.R.I.E.N.D.S.* He looked at me that way while handing me a cup of water.

"My mom thought we should stay a little longer. So she put the coffee on." He started to walk away once more. "I'm going to see if it's almost ready. Do you want me to take your cup in?"

I looked down. Every drop in the cup slurped up. "I didn't dump it, did I?"

"No, you've been drinking it." Steve laughed.

I wet my lips with my tongue. "I need more water." Gravity held me in place as I tried to stand. Finally, I reached my hand out. "Can you help me?"

He lifted my body without effort from the mesh prison. "I love you," I said.

His voice liquid in my ears, "I know, you tell me every time you smoke."

A splinter from aged floorboards pierced those words. Marriage meant commitment laughs in the dark, fights in the kitchen, kisses on the porch. At that moment, I felt like I consistently let him down. I could have cried on the floor, but I could have laughed at the moth circling the hanging light on the garage.

Steve sat me down on the couch in the living room. "I'll grab you coffee and some napkins," he kissed my lips, "just in case."

Frank held his hands over his chest. His thumbs twiddled in circular motions.

I spoke too loudly and too abruptly, "Hey, Gramps."

"Hey, what?"

"Whatcha been thinking about?" I asked.

"Oh, lots of things. Thanksgiving," he said.

"Thanksgiving?"

"Yeah, I can't remember if I ate today. Turkey, stuffing, and yams sound good. I didn't eat today, did I?" Frank asked.

"You ate, but not Thanksgiving," I laughed.

"Oh whoopie!" he said; then continued. "Did you know there was a Thanksgiving I almost lost everything?"

"I don't know if I've heard this story," I said.

"You know that Poppy's not my daughter, right?" Frank looked my way when he asked.

"I think I knew that." *Did I know?*

He spoke with clarity, "There was a time when I was too stubborn to realize how wonderful a child would be. I denied and denied my wife from a baby. Finally, she decided for both of us. We both did wrong, but I gave her no other choice." Frank stared at the blank TV. "So, we're gathered around the Thanksgiving table, and she handed me a slice of reality," he paused. "She served me divorce papers, and I shoved them up the turkey's ass."

The coffee cup nearly fell from my hands; hot liquid splashed onto my leg.

"It took us some time, but we both came around."

"How long did it take?" I asked.

"Not as long as it should have—about a year." Frank leaned back and twiddled his thumbs. "Poppy is my daughter."

Poppy came in with water and a cap of pills. "Alright dad, it's time to take your meds."

"Are they my love making pills?" Frank asked.

"No!" Poppy yelled, then laughed.

"I think all these pills fight each other when they reach my stomach. 'I do that.' 'No that's my job.' Do I have to take all of these?"

"You have to take them. I'll give you some ice cream if you take your pills," Poppy said.

Steve settled on the couch next to me; he twirled my hair around his fingers before he kissed my cheek. "Morgan, we should go home soon."

My head rested on his shoulder. "That's probably a good idea." I yawned. "I'm really sleepy."

"You remind me of a little kid," he joked. "Do you want me to carry you to the car?"

I pushed off him. "Not to the car, but you can carry me up the stairs." I giggled and kissed his cheek.

Poppy came back in with a mug of her own. Mother and son chatted, Gramps flipped on the TV, and I sat in silence. These people make up my family; they are not an extension; they are my family. Frank left Grams and Poppy, but he found his way back. I had no idea. It's incredible how thankful one could be for the time they have.

I felt guilty for so long; my Grandma died before I came home. I didn't say my final good-bye, or kiss her forehead, but I can talk her through thin air. My family missed me, but they are a phone call away. I am grateful for time.

Steve told me a story of this town when we moved in together; he warned me of the curse Kathleen placed on Claire Lake. For a long time, I truly believed it—I believed I was cursed to stay; not anymore. The story continues.

Steve drove us home passed the darkened trees hiding the lake.

Acknowledgements

I would like to thank my mom and Aunt Jan for the countless hours they listened to my stories and encouraged me to keep writing. Thank you to my best friend since the womb, Court. You have been inspiration to the pages written in this book and I couldn't have done this without you. Thank you to my wonderful husband that understood when I needed to empty my mind onto the page. I love you and could not have written these stories without you. There are so many who have inspired my work and imagination—teachers, dearest friends, family. Without the help and guidance of so many, this book would only be a dream.

CPSIA information can be obtained
at www.ICGtesting.com
Printed in the USA
LVHW111646190821
695554LV00003B/483